POWER PLAYS

Maureen Ulrich

COTEAU BOOKS FOR TEENS

Edited by Robert Currie.
Cover image: "Hockey Girl" by Paul Austring Photography.
Cover and book design by Duncan Campbell.
Printed and bound in Canada by AGMV Marquis.

Library and Archives Canada Cataloguing in Publication

Ulrich, Maureen, 1958-
      Power plays / Maureen Ulrich.

ISBN 978-1-55050-379-1

    I. Title.
PS8641.L75P69 2007   jC813'.6   C2007-904950-8

10 9 8 7 6 5 4 3 2 1

COTEAU
BOOKS
FOR TEENS

2517 Victoria Ave.
Regina, Saskatchewan
Canada   S4P 0T2

Available in Canada & the US from
Fitzhenry & Whiteside
195 Allstate Parkway
Markham, ON, L3R 4T8

The publisher gratefully acknowledges the financial support of its publishing program by: the Saskatchewan Arts Board, the Canada Council for the Arts, the Government of Canada through the Book Publishing Industry Development Program (BPIDP), Association for the Export of Canadian Books and the City of Regina Arts Commission.

 Canada Council for the Arts Conseil des Arts du Canada   SASKATCHEWAN ARTS BOARD Canada   Regina CITY OF REGINA

For Randy, Robin and Blaire,
and the girls and parents of the Estevan Xtreme.

chapter
one

I stare at the clock on the classroom wall. 3:27. Three minutes until two days of freedom. Mr. Wallis is droning on and on at the front of the class about our homework assignments for Monday. Then he rolls right into a lecture about the Halloween Dance at the Beefeater Hotel tonight and how we all have to behave and set a good example for Estevan Junior High. Everyone just smiles and nods because they've heard it all before. I haven't, but it doesn't matter. I wouldn't go to that dance if my life depended on it.

Believe it or not, Mr. Wallis is one of the few EJH teachers I like. He's usually in a good mood, and he tries to make his classes interesting. He uses cool expressions like "beware of Greeks bearing gifts" and "we're just two ships passing in the night." On the down side, he is obsessed with making us write out our daily assignments in our agendas.

Suddenly I realize that everyone's staring at me. What did I miss?

1

"Jessie, I don't see your agenda on your desk," Mr. Wallis is saying.

I start to reach under my chair to get it. As I do so, my plastic seat makes a squonking noise, just like a fart.

Of course this is timed perfectly with dead silence. You would have to be deaf not to hear it. Everyone starts to snicker and Derrick, who never hears anything Mr. Wallis says, starts laughing like a hyena. That really gets everyone going. While Mr. Wallis tries to regain control, I dig like a gopher in my backpack, pretending to look for my agenda. I can feel everyone's eyes burning holes in my back.

Mercifully Natalie Wilgenbush's cellphone starts playing Christina Aguilera's latest hit single, and Mr. Wallis makes a fuss because there's a school rule banning cell-phones – not that Natalie cares. She gives him this pathetic story about a family emergency, and he falls for it hook, line and sinker.

By the time I sit up, things are pretty much back to normal. And then I notice that Kim Scott is smiling at me. And not in a friendly way.

Why would she? She's definitely not my friend.

Still smiling, she deliberately pinches the end of her nose between her thumb and forefinger and squints her eyes. I scratch the bridge of my own nose with the tip of my middle finger and return the smile. That's for you, Bimbo.

When the bell rings, I hastily gather up my books and knapsack, determined to be the first one to leave.

"Jessie, I'd like to speak to you for a moment!" Mr. Wallis calls from across the room.

Great. While everybody files out, talking excitedly, I sink back into my seat. What now? Kim grins smugly as she cruises past.

When everyone is gone, Mr. Wallis closes the door. His plump face radiates concern as he leans over my desk. Here we go again, I think to myself. Fireside Chat Number Seven.

"I'm worried about you," he says abruptly.

I'm sure he is. Frankly I'm a little worried myself, but there's no way I'm telling him that. I make a deliberate effort not to look at the door, where Derrick and Jason are standing on tiptoe with their faces pressed against the rectangular window at the top.

"Have you made any friends since you moved here?"

I give him a big smile. "The girls in this school are stuck-up."

Mr. Wallis raises an eyebrow, then picks up a brush and busily begins erasing the whiteboard, which is scrawled with Norse mythology notes. I know I've ticked him off. When the board is empty — and I say empty because it's never clean, he turns and says, "I know it's tough making an adjustment to a new city and a new school. Adolescence can be a difficult time for students, and it can be especially difficult..."

As he rambles on, I cross my arms and stare at the graffiti on the cover of my English binder, which is, in my humble opinion, a work of art. My three best friends in Saskatoon used to draw pictures on it. Bailey's cartoon is my favourite. She sketched a dairy cow's rear end with the head looking back over its left shoulder. There's a huge bubble coming out of its mouth saying: "Luv ya, J!" Keisha, Tayja, and I became best buds in kindergarten. Keisha and I have played ringette together since we were six. Then Bailey moved next door to me in Grade Five and our trio became a quartet. Mr. Oldershaw, our Grade Eight homeroom teacher, called us "the Fab Four."

When I look up again, Mr. Wallis has placed the brush back on the ledge and is staring at me. "When you first arrived, there were a number of girls, including Kim, who tried to be friendly."

I'd like to tell him that Kim and Natalie and the rest of the girls in this class have him wrapped around their little fingers, but I don't.

"The staff is very concerned about you — especially Mr. Kowalski."

I give him a shrug to indicate my lack of concern for Mr. Kowalski's feelings. The man makes us copy pages of notes — day after day. My hand is throbbing by the end of the class. Aren't we supposed to do experiments in science?

Mr. Wallis rests his round bottom on the edge of the desk and clasps his hands around his bent knee. "You were in a gifted program last year. But you now appear content with 70s. You go home every day for lunch, and you don't take part in extracurriculars. Wouldn't you like to get the most out of Grade Nine before you head off to the Comp next year?"

Yeah, well if I still lived in Saskatoon, I'd be in Walter Murray Collegiate, and we would not be having this conversation.

He takes a deep breath and launches into a long speech on the importance of adaptation to a new environment and what it means to have school spirit and a bunch of other stuff I don't pay much attention to.

When he stops to take a breath, I abruptly stand up and stuff my books into my backpack. "Can I go home now?" I ask him. "I have to babysit my sister." That's a lie, because Courtney figure skates after school every weekday.

"Of course." He looks hurt, but he steps aside so I can pass. "Have a nice weekend. We'll talk again on Monday."

Don't count on it.

The hallway is vacant. I throw my backpack on the floor and open my locker, grabbing my blue hoodie. As soon as I start to pull it over my head, I notice the huge brown stain, still wet. My binders and textbooks are soaked too.

Crap! Somebody's poured Coke on my stuff – again.

I wipe up the mess as best I can with my hoodie and dig through the bottom of my locker in search of a plastic shopping bag. In the process, I find my ringette jacket, which I quit wearing weeks ago. At least it's dry, and since it's too cold to walk home in my t-shirt, I put it on. I shove my English books and agenda in the top of my locker, then roll up the hoodie and stuff it in my backpack, which I throw over my shoulder. I slam the locker shut and reattach the combination lock, even though it's pretty much useless because Kim and Natalie obviously know my combination.

Instead of using the Grade Nine entrance at the front, I head for the main staircase, thinking that I'll duck out the gym doors at the back of the school. What a stroke of luck that the only person I encounter along the way is Mr. Saxon, the custodian. As I hurry down the steps leading to the gym, the sounds of laughter and squeaky gym shoes drift upwards. One of the volleyball teams must be practising.

When I turn the corner, I nearly run into three girls standing beside the pop machine. They're all wearing gym shorts and t-shirts and holding bottles of Gatorade. The one with her back to me is Kim. I thought I recognized her laugh. Another is tall and broad-shouldered with her long, blonde hair pulled up in a ponytail. The third one has a slight build and short, dark, very curly hair.

"He had a lot of good players to pick from," the dark-haired girl is saying. "Maybe you didn't have a good tryout."

"Are you kidding? Jodi Palmer made that team because her dad's the coach!"

Ah yes, everyone in our class knows about the global conspiracy to keep Kim off the Bantam AA boys' hockey team.

I try to walk around them without being noticed, but Kim immediately calls out, "Hey, Jessie, how come you're not wearing your hoodie?" The sarcasm in her voice is unmistakable.

I shrug my shoulders. "None of your business," I reply. I try to step around her, but she moves too fast.

"Going to the dance tonight?" Kim asks.

"I have to stay home and babysit my sister."

"That's too bad. You really should get out more, Jessie. Get involved in school activities."

Wouldn't she just love that?

The dark-haired girl points at the crest on my jacket. "You play ringette?" she asks.

"Used to."

I try to squeeze between them, but the tall blonde says, "You're the new girl, right? What's your name again?"

"Jessie McIntyre."

That's right. Six weeks later and I'm still the "new girl." And probably will be until somebody else comes along. I hope it's soon.

"I heard you're a good setter. How come you didn't try out for the volleyball team?" the dark-haired girl asks.

Kim laughs in a nasty sort of way, but I ignore her. "I moved here after tryouts," I reply. Where did she hear about my setting? I'm lucky if I can get through a PE class without having a ball served at my head.

"That's too bad. We could have used you. Kim here sucks at passing," the blonde says, punching Kim lightly in the shoulder.

Kim's face turns red. "Maybe you'd like to try winning at districts without me!" She screws the lid back on her Gatorade and walks off in a huff.

"Whoa, who peed in her cornflakes?" The dark girl turns to me. "Hey, Jessie. I'm Tara Brewer and this is Shauna Langley. We're in 217."

"Nice to meet you."

I say it, but I don't mean it. This whole thing could just be another set-up. Like the time Kim got Nicole Brown, one of the girls in Room 216, to hang out with me after school. Thanks to Nicole, Kim had enough information to humiliate me for a week.

"Ever think about playing hockey, instead of ringette?" Shauna asks, exchanging glances with Tara.

What did I tell you? Another set-up.

"Ever seen a ringette game?" I challenge her.

"Two teams from Saskatoon and Regina did a clinic here a few years ago, and I watched for a while. It looked like fun." Shauna quickly adds, "But I wouldn't be caught dead doing it. Kind of like riding a moped — when you can ride a motorcycle."

"Are you girls coming to practice or not?" an adult voice demands.

The three of us look over at Ms. Franklin, who stands at the gym entrance, hands resting on her hips and whistle dangling from her neck.

"Sure, Coach," Shauna says quickly, heading for the gym.

Tara is close on her heels. "Bye, Jessie. Talk to you again."

Not if I can help it.

The crisp October air chills me as I step outside, but the sun is warm on my face. I cut across the school grounds and head east along the road which winds like a snake beside the edge of the valley. The baseball diamonds below are deserted.

The sun glints on the holding ponds just past the diamonds, and the prairie landscape beyond is pimpled with brown spill piles, remnants of the coal strip mining operation. The Shand and Boundary power stations puff streams of white smoke across a pale blue sky. I try not to look at the Shand, where my dad now works as an electrical engineer.

"I know this move will be hard for you," he told me after he accepted a SaskPower transfer last May, "but you'll have the entire summer to adjust. Maybe you can play some softball and make some new friends. By the time you start Grade Nine in the fall, you'll be glad we moved."

He lied. We didn't arrive in Estevan until the second week of classes.

Two blocks from the school, there's a small playground and paddling pool, which overlook the valley. I like to stop there on my way home. School gets out earlier in Estevan than it does in Saskatoon, so there's no point in going on MSN until after four o'clock. I move to the south side of the brick change shack, so I can't be seen from the street, then shrug off my backpack and dig out last year's agenda from a zippered pocket on the side. Sitting down, I open the agenda and start flipping the pages. Every square centimeter is covered with notes Tayja, Bailey, Keisha and I wrote to each other during math class, like:

J-girl ur 2 kewl Isaac thnks ur hot cul8r K

I should show this to Mr. Wallis. Then he'd know what an agenda is for.

When Mr. Wallis introduced me to my homeroom, I felt like a total geek. I just knew everyone was staring at my mouth, which is way too large for my face. I wore my Stars jacket because I thought it would give me status.

I was so wrong.

The girls in my homeroom were nice enough at first. They were curious about Saskatoon, mainly wanting to know what the boys were like. Kim never said much. She just watched and listened while I babbled on and on about "the Fab Four" and Hugh Cairns Elementary and volleyball and ringette and softball. I must have sounded like an idiot.

The boys gave me a lot of attention too, and I guess I let that go to my head. I started going out with Riley the first week, then switched to Jason the next. My second major mistake. Suddenly the girls got all protective of "poor Riley." Natalie Wilgenbush told me that Kim called me a tease, and I dissed Kim right to Natalie's face. Mistake number three. Natalie just happens to be the biggest mouth at EJH and Kim Scott's BFF. Thanks to MSN, word of my faux pas reached the Kremlin by nightfall.

The next day the girls stopped talking to me and started talking ABOUT me. I didn't eat lunch at school because I had to walk Courtney home at noon and make her a sandwich. Noon is an important time at EJH. The students who stay at noon eat together in the gym and then go outside for twenty minutes to socialize. Everything happens at lunch. The flirting. The rumours. The breakups.

At first, I begged my mom to let me take a lunch, but she said I needed to look after Courtney. My mom can't seem to get used to the fact that Estevan is a much safer city than Saskatoon. She's way too protective of both Courtney and me. She won't let me have my own cellphone or computer or get a part-time job. And I can only go on MSN for one hour a day. That really sucks.

In the end, it turned out to be a good thing that I didn't eat lunch at school because I wouldn't have anyone to sit with anyway. For a while, the girls in my class pretty much ignored me.

And then things started to happen.

My shirt ended up in the toilet during PE class. My pencil case kept getting ripped off. Feet suddenly appeared in the aisle, tripping me. Nasty notes showed up in my locker. *Brown-noser!* they said. *Suck-up!* I quit trying to get good grades.

I know Kim is behind it all. She never misses the chance to stab me in the back.

Because of her comments on MSN, I blocked everybody except for my friends from Saskatoon and my cousins in Ontario. And I stopped accepting emails from Kim and her pals weeks ago.

I close the agenda and carefully return it to my backpack, then head for home. A pair of little girls rides past me on their bikes, giggling and talking in their high-pitched voices. Suddenly I feel very tired.

What did I ever do to make Kim hate me so much?

chapter two

That night I take Courtney out trick-or-treating for a few hours after supper, then make us both a cup of hot chocolate. While Mom and Dad are upstairs getting ready for a costume party, I turn on the computer in the kitchen, hoping I can catch one of the Fab Four at home.

Mom comes downstairs and stops in front of the hallway mirror, tucking her blonde hair under a silly blue hat. "I feel guilty making you stay home and babysit tonight," she says, without looking at me. "Isn't there some place you'd rather be?"

"No," I lie. Actually I'd rather be just about anywhere but Estevan. I've become really good at lying to my parents lately. Sometimes it scares me.

She smooths out the wrinkles on her matching blue blazer and skirt, then pops her cellphone inside her clutch. "Would you like to guess who I am?"

I take a sip of my hot chocolate. "I don't have a clue."

"Maybe you need a stronger hint." Walking towards the stairs, she calls out, "John, are you nearly ready? It's seven thirty!"

"Coming!"

I follow Mom into the living room. At first all I can hear is Courtney laughing and giggling excitedly. I feel a premonition of disaster. Then, through the railing, a pair of red boots and blue tights comes into view.

"Doesn't Daddy look funny?" Courtney squeals, peering out from behind the red cape that floats down from Dad's shoulders.

"What are you wearing?" I ask, horrified.

"Your mother dyed a pair of my long underwear, and I found these red jogging shorts at the Salvation Army," Dad replies proudly.

I stare at Dad, horrified. The shorts are far too tight and his stomach protrudes over the waistband like a flat tire. He looks like a total dork.

"I rented the cape at that costume place on Thirteenth Avenue." Mom adjusts the cape across Dad's shoulders. "And I sewed the emblem myself. What do you think, Jessie?"

"You're not going to walk out of the house dressed like that!" I exclaim.

Superman smiles confidently and flexes both biceps. "How else am I supposed to leap tall buildings in a single bound? And protect Lois Lane from the forces of evil?" He grabs Mom and squeezes her until she shrieks with laughter.

I hate it when they act like teenagers. "Just don't let anybody see you," I plead. "I put up with enough crap at school as it is."

"What do you mean?" Mom looks worried all of a sudden.

"Just kidding," I say quickly. The last thing I need is Mom marching into the principal's office and demanding a conference with the EJH staff. With any luck, if I can just stay under the radar for a while, this thing with Kim will blow over in a few weeks."

I worry about you sometimes, Jessie." She puts her hands on my shoulders and squeezes. "Why don't you invite some girls from your class over sometime? You could have a sleep-over or something."

Right.

"Not that we want you inviting people over when we're not home. Remember what happened last time?"

Yeah, I remember. I tried to have a little "going away" party in Saskatoon this summer, and a whole bunch of high school kids showed up. It was a disaster.

After Mom and Dad leave, I watch television while Courtney arranges and rearranges her candy into neat piles. Mom has strict rules about not eating too many sweets. When Courtney's constant shuffling begins to annoy me, I tell her it's bedtime.

"But it's not a school night!" Courtney wipes her hand across her mouth and smears her black moustache all the way up to her ear. "Mom lets me stay up to at least ten o'clock on a Friday night! And it's Halloween too!" She searches for a suitable bribe. "Want a popcorn ball? Or some taffy?"

"No thanks. Get ready for bed. I'll let you watch a scary movie with me if you promise not to tell Mom and Dad I let you stay up."

"Wahoo!" Courtney darts up the stairs and disappears into her bedroom on the second level.

The doorbell rings.

Through the translucent glass in the door, I can see the bright colours of Halloween costumes. When I open it, Tara Brewer is standing on my front step, accompanied by a small green dragon and a larger red devil. They are both holding bright orange pumpkins and shivering.

"Hi, Jessie!" Tara says brightly. "Kim said you lived here, but I wasn't sure. This used to be the Blackburns' house."

Kim knows where I live? Terrific. Does that mean all the stuff going on at school is going to follow me home?

"Well, it's our house now." I reach for a handful of suckers and taffy.

"This is my brother Jeffrey and my sister Katelyn." Tara gestures to the devil and the dragon in turn. "As you can see, Jeffrey isn't dressing up this year."

"Ha, ha," says Jeffrey emphatically.

The green dragon yawns. "I'm cold, Tara. Let's go home."

"This is our last stop, Kate." Tara pulls her sister against her legs and hugs her.

"Here you go." I drop the candy into the waiting pumpkins, which are nearly overflowing.

Tara gives me a curious look. "Couldn't you get out of babysitting so you could go to the Halloween Dance? It's the best dance of the year."

"I didn't feel like going anyway."

"My mom phoned the school to get me a late pass. She has to work at the hospital tonight, and Dad's on duty too. Which is why I got stuck taking the rug rats Halloweening." She nods her head in the direction of the street where a minivan is parked. "When we go home, my grandma's going to babysit, so I can go to the dance."

"Is your dad a cop or something?"

"RCMP," Tara says. "There was a lot of vandalism in Lignite last year, so I hope he won't be too busy."

Tara seems really nice. Still, it's too much of a coincidence that she's on my doorstep right now. She's probably going to report to Kim as soon as she gets to the dance.

Jeffrey announces, "This is boring." He turns and saunters down the sidewalk toward the van.

"Tara, let's go!" Katelyn whines.

"Can't you see I'm talking to someone?" Tara picks up her little sister and places her on her hip. "I won't be able to stay for the whole dance. We play volleyball in Weyburn tomorrow, and hockey starts Sunday."

"You play hockey too?" I ask, surprised.

Tara nods. "I play Bantam girls — with Shauna. We also have girls from the Catholic schools and from out of town. There's only nine of us so far. We'll have to pull up some Peewees to make a team."

"I didn't know there was girls' hockey here." Although I don't understand why, my heart starts to race.

"This is my fourth year on a girls' team," Tara explains. "The problem is some of the really good girl hockey players — like Kim Scott and Jodi Palmer — play on guys' teams. We never got Shauna until last year and Jennifer and Carla until this year." She shifts Katelyn to her other hip. "Why don't you come to our practice on Sunday?"

"I don't have the right equipment," I quickly reply. "Besides, it's probably too late to join."

"Let's go!" Katelyn demands, smacking Tara on the arm.

"Think it over!" Tara shouts over her shoulder as Katelyn waves a small green mitten in my direction.

I absent-mindedly return the wave and retreat to the house, still shivering. Courtney, now swaddled in pajamas, slippers and a housecoat, is back on the living room floor, staring in disgust at her pile of chocolate bars.

"You took some, didn't you?" Her brown eyes are accusing.

"Don't be paranoid." I resume my place on the couch and pick up the remote from the end table.

"What's paranoid?"

"Never mind. Come sit with me."

I flick through the stations until Courtney and I agree on a movie, but as we watch it, my mind keeps drifting back to my conversation with Tara. Why haven't I heard anything about girls' hockey in Estevan? There were lots of girls' teams in Saskatoon, but because I was too busy with ringette and school sports, I never considered joining. There were at least two girls on the Stars who played hockey and ringette – and they were really good at both.

Would I be any good at hockey? I wonder. No. Those bulky hockey pants would be uncomfortable, and I'd have to learn new rules. It would be embarrassing to be so far behind the other players.

By the time the movie ends, Courtney is snoring softly with her head on my lap. It's nearly ten o'clock and Mom and Dad won't be home for at least two hours. Maybe Keisha will be on MSN. I carry Courtney up to her bedroom and tuck her in.

The front doorbell rings and then rings three more times before I get back downstairs.

Instead of trick-or-treaters, there is a short, heavy-set girl standing on my doorstep. I have never seen her before. Her spiky hair is dyed black and burgundy, and her right eyebrow and lower lip are pierced. Her dark eyes are coated with eyeliner and mascara. She plants her hand on my chest and shoves me back into the living room. "Happy to see me?" she crows.

Then she barges right into my house.

I'm too shocked to stop her. My heart's pounding like crazy. It's like being invaded by a piledriver reeking of beer and stale smoke.

She bellows over her shoulder. "Tyler, hurry up!"

There's more of them?

Tyler turns out to be short, scrawny and at least seventeen. Staggering through the door with a nearly empty bottle of Crown Royal in his hand, he has a baseball cap jammed backwards on his shaven head and a scraggly goatee.

Tipping back the bottle of Crown Royal, he takes a final swig. "Nice place." He wipes his mouth, then hiccups loudly. "Lots nicer than Marsha's dump."

The girl swears at him, then thrusts her head out the door. "Where's Rick? I thought I told both of you to come inside."

There's three?

"Takin' a leak," Tyler says.

I finally find my voice. "Who *are* you?"

He grins stupidly and wags a finger in my direction. "You may not know me, but you know Marsha!"

Marsha's reddened eyes are glistening with pure hatred. I swear I've never seen her before, can't imagine what's made her so mad.

I hope my voice isn't going to shake. "Do you go to EJH?" I ask.

"As if!" Marsha explodes. "I got out of that dump three years ago!"

"So you go to ECS." I attempt to make normal conversation. "I don't know any students who go there. You see, I just moved here and —"

"I don't want to hear your frickin' life story!" Marsha interrupts, slamming the door. "I just want to know why you think you can get away with calling me a fat pig!"

My heart shifts into high gear. "I've never seen you before!" I protest. "And even if I had, I wouldn't call you that!"

"You're a liar!" Marsha shouts. "Maybe I should show you what happens to little rich girls who trash-talk me!"

A small voice from upstairs calls out, "Jessie, who's there?"

"Nobody! Go back to sleep!"

"Maybe Little Sister would like to come down and party with us." Tyler heads towards the stairs, navigating my living room as if it's tilted at a forty-five degree angle.

"Please don't go up there," I beg. "She's only eight."

Fortunately, Tyler is overcome by a spell of vertigo and collapses on the first step. "Whoa!" He holds his head in both his hands, then promptly places it between his knees and pukes on the carpet.

Marsha begins to laugh hysterically.

"Jessie!" comes Courtney's voice again.

"Courtney, don't you dare come down!" I'm getting desperate.

"No wonder you're getting sick, Tyler! Look at all that puke in you!" Marsha says.

I start pleading with her. "Look, I honestly don't know who you are. And I have no idea why you think I was calling you names. But my parents are on their way home right now. Please, you've got to go."

She just keeps on laughing while Tyler pukes his guts out.

Suddenly the doorbell rings and keeps on ringing. I feel like I'm living in the horror movie Courtney and I were just watching. I open the door, hoping to find one of my neighbours, but the guy standing on my front step taking nervous tokes from his cigarette is a total stranger. He has a scruffy black mullet and his denim jacket is several sizes too small and ripped in the shoulders.

He pushes past me, his eyes darting about the room. "Where's Marsha?" he demands.

"Welcome to the party, Rick!" Marsha shouts cheerfully. Laughing, she flops down on the couch and props her heavy black boots on the coffee table.

I have to get them out of here. "There's no party here."

Rick looks over my shoulder at Tyler. "Hey man, I told you to go easy on that whiskey!"

"Tyler's not feeling very well. Maybe you should take him home."

Tyler groans and pukes again. The foul smell makes me feel like puking too.

Marsha smiles triumphantly at me. "Rick, this is the piece of crap who's been spreading rumours about me. The one I've been wanting to punch out."

Punch out? I stare at Marsha's fleshy knuckles.

"Whatever." Rick takes a drag from his cigarette. "You just said you wanted to stop here for a few minutes. I didn't know you planned to stay."

Marsha grins at me. "Mommy and Daddy aren't home. Good time to have us a house-wrecker."

An image comes to mind. My house — full of drunken strangers — with Courtney scared out of her mind. There has to be some way to get them out of here before they kick the crap out of my living room — and me. I try to think of an excuse to go to the kitchen, so I can call Mom on her cell.

The guttural sounds of Tyler's dry heaves provide some inspiration.

"I'll get Tyler a glass of water and a towel." I start backing towards the kitchen.

Rick grabs my arm, halting me in my tracks. "Got any booze?"

I can't let them at my parents' liquor.

"Come on." Rick gives my arm a little shake. "Just give us some booze."

"There might be some in the liquor cabinet. I'll show you if you promise to leave."

"Where is it?" Marsha demands.

I walk over to the entertainment centre and open it, exposing enough liquor to keep them drunk for a week.

Rick starts doing inventory with Marsha looking over his shoulder. She removes the lid from a bottle of Silent Sam and takes a glug while Rick stuffs a forty of rye under one arm and a twenty-six of amber rum under the other.

"My parents will be home soon." I hope I sound convincing.

Rick peers out the curtains veiling the picture window. "Marsha, let's get outta here."

Marsha laughs derisively. "Are you afraid?"

I'm pretty sure she's talking to Rick — not me. I feel a clammy hand on my arm and realize that Tyler is right beside me, reeking of stale sweat and smoke and vomit. He holds a crumpled pack of cigarettes in his hand. He fumbles with the foil and shoves the open package at me. Several joints are poking out.

"Want to get a buzz on?" he offers.

"No thanks," I reply automatically.

"You know what you need to do, rich girl?" He breathes sour fumes in my face. "You need to relax."

That's when the cellphone in his jacket pocket starts playing a Metallica tune. He flips it open and closes one eye in order to read the text message. "Everybody's leaving the 7-Eleven," he informs the others. When he tries to slip his cellphone back in his pocket, he loses his balance and stumbles against the table in our entryway, upsetting the lamp. It smashes into a billion pieces on the ceramic tile.

Great.

Marsha starts cackling again.

"Sorry." Tyler grins at me sheepishly. Considering what Marsha is planning to do to my house, his apology sounds ridiculous.

"I'm going to that bonfire in Lignite," Rick announces, dropping his cigarette butt and using the toe of his boot to grind it into the carpet. Crap! What's Mom going to do when she sees that? "Are you two coming or not?"

"No! We're partying here!" Marsha sits defiantly on the couch and tips back the Silent Sam.

"Suit yourself." Rick shrugs and heads towards the door.

He's going to leave? Without Marsha and Tyler? I have to stop him.

"Do you have another cigarette, Rick?" I call out.

He turns and stares at me as if he's seeing me for the first time, then hands me the two liquor bottles. He removes a cigarette from the breast pocket of his jean jacket and lights it between his own lips before handing it to me. Humphrey Bogart couldn't be more gallant.

I hand him the bottle of rye and take the cigarette with shaking fingers. Two years ago, I smoked a cigarette with Tayja, but I didn't like it much. I inhale a little and nearly choke.

"Thanks," I croak, stifling a cough.

"Wanna come along?" he asks.

My eyes are watering. "I'd really like to, but I can't." I glance at the stairs. "My little sister —"

Marsha jumps to her feet. "You're not going anywhere!"

"Come on, Marsh," Tyler whines. "We're gonna miss the bonfire if we hang out here."

Marsha cusses him out.

Unperturbed, Tyler stumbles over to the entertainment center and stocks up on my dad's expensive Scotch and liqueurs.

Rick slips an arm around my shoulders and removes the cigarette from my fingers. "Haven't you had enough already?" he asks Tyler, taking a drag.

"Gonna make me some fancy drinks," Tyler slurs, weaving back across the living room, his arms full of bottles. He fumbles with the front door a while before finally getting it open. He staggers out. It'll be a miracle if he can negotiate the steps without falling.

"Looks like you're gonna be partying by yourself, Marsha," Rick says.

Marsha starts swearing at Rick now. I've never even heard some of the words she uses, but it doesn't seem to bother Rick at all.

"Let's go, Marsha," he says. "Tyler's got enough booze to last us a week." He heads towards the door, pulling me along with him. Small chance now of getting both of them out the door and locking it behind them so I can call one of the neighbours.

A sudden shove from behind propels me through the threshold and onto the front step. Obviously Marsha has changed her mind about staying. I knock over one of Mom's empty planters and drop the bottle of rum, which shatters on the cement. Marsha just walks past me and heads for the car, a brand new bottle of vodka in her hand.

Rick looks about in agitation, but the street — unfortunately — appears deserted. Many of the houses are dark.

"Nice job, Marsha," he says.

"Well, go get some more!" Marsha snaps back.

"We got enough. Let's just get outta here." He closes the front door behind him and descends the steps, his boots grinding the glass to powder. He grabs my arm — almost gently — and pulls me along with him towards the jacked up Camaro parked in our driveway. The air feels cold, and I suddenly realize I don't have a jacket.

Tyler is already snoring in the back seat. Marsha shoves me in beside him, then climbs in the front. What's going to happen to me? And Courtney?

Rick stares at me in the rear-view mirror as he inserts the ignition key. "Why don't you smile?" he asks. "Aren't you having a good time?"

"She's having the time of her life!" Marsha laughs. "Can't you tell?" She turns around, her teeth and eyebrow ring winking in the darkness. "And just wait till she meets the rest of the gang!"

My blood freezes.

"Enough threats," Rick says quietly.

We head east — out of the city. The trip to Lignite is terrifying. Driving way over the speed limit, Rick passes one car on the shoulder and pulls out to pass another while meeting a semi, veering back into our lane just in time. Tyler is dead to the world, snoring like a chainsaw, while Marsha guzzles vodka and talks non-stop the whole way about what her friends are going to do to me when we get to Lignite. Rick tells her a few times to shut up. Will he protect me when we get there?

Bales of straw are blazing in the middle of the street in Lignite. A huge bonfire is burning at the campground, and dozens of young people are drinking and tossing picnic tables into the flames. It's worse than a horror movie.

Rick parks across from the campground and climbs out of the car. "Looks like we got here just in time for the party," he says, looking down at me. "Let's go, rich girl."

chapter three

I stare gloomily at the tile beneath my feet and the steel bars beyond. A thunderous snore from the next cell startles me, and I glance for the hundredth time at the clock on the wall. One thirty a.m. Why is Mom taking so long? I tap my fingers impatiently on the edge of the cot.

For a panicky moment, I wonder if either of my parents will come. Is Courtney okay? Do they think I took all that booze? I can't imagine spending the night here. The last time I was in a police station I was touring it with Mrs. McGillivray and my Grade One class. How can this be happening to me?

I feel a momentary pang as I think about Courtney left alone in the house. She must have been terrified. She probably thought I was kidnapped or something.

And Marsha. I'm sure I'd never seen her before. Where did she hear that I'd called her a fat pig? I smile, recalling how well the description fit her upturned snout.

"Jessie?"

I look up to see Constable Brewer standing on the other side of the bars. Wouldn't you just guess it would be the father of someone I know who carts me off to jail? He has removed his cap, which has left a red ridge on his wide forehead. He has dark blue eyes and black, close-cropped hair, the same colour as Tara's. The resemblance between them is striking, apart from his huge frame and the black handlebar mustache beneath his hawk-like nose.

"Jessie, before your mother gets here, I want you to tell me who drove you to Lignite."

I shake my head. No way am I pissing off Marsha even more. There's no telling what she'd do if she had a real reason to be mad at me.

The constable sighs. "It'll go much easier for you if you just tell me the names of your friends. You're in a lot of trouble already. Do you really want to shoulder all the blame for the vandalism to that house?"

A wave of panic breaks over me. "No!"

"That's a step in the right direction. What can you tell me?"

"I didn't know the guy who was driving."

"Can you tell me anything about him?"

"He had black hair." I wonder if I should tell him about Tyler and the drugs, then decide against it. "I didn't really notice much. I was too scared."

Constable Brewer pulls a small leather notepad out of his breast pocket, flips a few pages, and jots some notes. His fingers are the size of bananas. "Was anyone else in the vehicle?"

My head spins as I consider my answer. Should I say "No one" or try to make someone up?

"Why are you afraid, Jessie?"

Hot tears are filming my eyes. I wipe my nose with my jacket sleeve.

"They won't know you told me. This is just between you and me."

"Of course they'll know! Even if you find out from someone else, they'd still think I narked on them! People saw me leaving in your cruiser. By the time I go back to school on Monday, everybody'll know everything."

"And what they don't know, they'll make up," the constable adds. "Maybe you better pick some new friends."

"I can't help it! Marsha picked me!"

Crap!

Constable Brewer is already scribbling on his notepad. "Marsha Schultz." He shakes his head in disgust. "The city police have run her in half a dozen times for assault, theft and vandalism. She kicked a pregnant girl in the abdomen a few months ago. How nice for me she's taken her show on the road."

She kicked a pregnant girl? I feel sick to my stomach.

The officer arches one black eyebrow, then taps the pen thoughtfully against his front teeth. "Now let me see. How about Tyler Holm? Does that name sound familiar?"

I forget my fear as I stare at him in amazement. "How do you know so much?"

He raps his red-ringed forehead with a large knuckle. "It helps to have a photographic memory for names and faces. You may have noticed my cranial cavity is rather large."

I can't help but smile.

"As for Marsha and Tyler, I'll run them in next week and concoct a story about how I came up with their names." He returns the notepad to his breast pocket. "Why don't you get some sleep? I don't think you're going to get much at home."

I nod and wipe my eyes again. Suddenly I feel very tired.

"Take my advice. Find yourself some new pals. I don't want to see you in here again."

When he's gone, I stretch out on the cot and stare at the ceiling, trying to sleep. But my traitorous mind keeps replaying the events of the evening.

I didn't want to get out of ... car, but Marsha kept yanking on my arm, so eventually I climbed out. Tyler was still passed out in the back seat. It was so cold I actually thought about going nearer to that bonfire to warm up.

By then Rick had opened the trunk and started taking

out cartons of eggs and canisters of spray paint. He shoved a canister in my hand.

I stared at it in disbelief.

"I thought we were going to the bonfire!" Marsha shouted. "The girls want to kick her ass!"

"Maybe later," Rick said. "Let's raise some hell first."

The two of them advanced on an innocent bungalow with a neatly manicured yard and a grinning jack-o'-lantern on the front doorstep. The windows were dark, and the driveway empty of vehicles. Rick wasted no time in spraying the F-word on the front door and egging the windows. Marsha kicked the jack-o'-lantern to pieces, scattering orange shards in the flower bed. A couple of kids at the bonfire noticed what they were doing and cheered. Rick and Marsha waved in acknowledgment and started to move down the block.

I saw my opportunity for escape. I could just run to one of the houses and knock on the door. Surely somebody would let me in.

Marsha turned and yelled at me from across the yard. "What are you waiting for?"

Waiting for you to forget about me, I felt like saying. Reluctantly, I started to walk across the lawn towards her. I was half-frozen by then.

That's when two RCMP cruisers showed up, red and blue lights pulsing. One drove in from the north end of the street while the other came from the south. The kids drinking at the campground just stood and watched. They didn't even seem concerned. Marsha pelted one of the cruisers with an egg before running between two houses. Rick jumped into the Camaro and drove right across the lawn, narrowly missing a tree. He went squealing down the street with one of the cruisers in pursuit. Meanwhile I bolted towards the cop car left behind.

Forgetting that I had a can of spray paint in my hand.

But I didn't care. At least I was safe.

After the RCMP officers were done handing out tickets to the kids in the campground, they took me and a lippy twelve-year-old boy back to the detachment. We were questioned, our parents contacted, and then taken to cells to wait. The boy's father arrived an hour ago. He didn't even look that upset when he dragged his son out of here.

The cell thing seems a little harsh. After all I'm not really a criminal.

Where are my parents?

chapter four

n hour later, I am sitting on the couch in my own living room, waiting for my dad to finish his rant and let me go to bed. I'm so tired I'm nearly seeing double. White noise is buzzing in my ears.

And frankly it's really hard to take someone seriously when he's wearing a Superman costume. There are huge saggy wrinkles around his knees, and when he paces, his cape sort of floats out behind him like he's flying. He looks dorkier than ever.

The broken lamp has been cleaned up, and Tyler's puke is gone – although the smell still lingers. I'd like to ask who did the honours, but I don't have the nerve. Probably not Dad. His stomach is too weak. I don't know how he ever changed diapers.

I suddenly realize that Dad has stopped pacing and is staring at me. Waiting for an apology perhaps?

"I'm sorry."

"You're sorry! We come home to find your little sister in hysterics, puke all over the floor, and half our booze missing, and you say you're sorry? Well, young lady, sorry isn't good enough!" Dad rages. "Have you thought about what might have happened to Courtney – left all alone – or what might have happened to you in that riot?"

I stifle a yawn before replying. "It wasn't a riot. And I told you, I didn't go there by choice. Why won't you believe me?"

"You want us to believe three total strangers walked into our house on Halloween night and kidnapped you?" he demands. "One of the neighbours saw you come stumbling out of the house with your arms full of booze. She says you just got in that car and drove away!"

"Did it ever occur to you that's not what she saw?"

"Don't take that patronizing tone with me, young lady! It's perfectly obvious to your mother and me that there was some sort of *party* going on here! Puke on the carpet, a lamp broken, cigarette burns, a bottle of booze shattered on the front step! When did you start hanging out with this kind of crowd?"

I know it looks bad, but why won't he believe me? "I told you, I'm not hanging out with them."

"Daddy, I can't sleep!" comes a tired voice from upstairs.

Mom stands at the front window, her back turned towards me. "John, go to bed. All of us are exhausted."

Dad shakes his head and continues pacing.

"You're going to say something that you'll regret. Talk to her tomorrow."

Dad abruptly stops and rubs his forehead and eyes. "All right." He heads towards the stairs, then calls over his shoulder. "You have definitely not heard the last word from me!"

Probably not. But with any luck, I'll get a few hours sleep before Round Two.

I look hopefully at Mom, thinking that maybe she'll follow him. She takes a deep breath and launches into her own version of the same lecture.

"Ever since we moved here, I've made excuses for you and put up with your moods. I know this move has been hard on you, but tonight you went too far. Whatever that judge decides for you in terms of community service, you will do it – every second – and pay every penny. You're also going to pay for every drop of booze stolen from our liquor cabinet." She turns and stares at me with tired eyes. "I've reached the end of my rope. I won't allow your stupidity to put your little sister at risk."

"I was trying to protect her!" I pick up a cushion and hug it tightly. "Haven't you been listening? I've told you a hundred times!" I can't stop the yawn this time. "I went with Marsha so she wouldn't wreck our house."

"You left an eight-year-old girl here alone so you could go to a party." Mom adds bitterly, "I hope you had a great time."

"I didn't have a great time! While we were driving to Lignite, I thought we were going to hit the ditch — or have a head-on collision!"

"Exaggerating the danger will not get my sympathy —"

"I'm not exaggerating!"

"Start taking responsibility for your actions because I am sick to death of your excuses and your attitude! Good night."

I watch her until she reaches the top of the stairs, then stretch out on the couch and bury my face in the cushion. What's the matter with them? They never even listened to me.

I spend the following afternoon doing fall yardwork and washing walls while Mom visits the RCMP detachment. When she returns, she says nothing, waiting until supper to give us the good news.

"You what?" Dad asks incredulously.

Mom sets a platter of barbecued pork chops in front of him. "You heard me. I signed up Jessie for girls' hockey."

Dad shakes his head. "Now how is that supposed to help?"

Ignoring him, Mom turns to me. "What do you think about the idea?"

"You should have asked me first." I stare at my empty plate and trace the floral pattern with my fingertip.

"I wanna play girls' hockey," Courtney pipes up.

I shoot her a scathing look. "You can't play hockey!"

"Why not?" Courtney tilts her chin, as if prepared to dig in and fight. "I can skate as good as you can!"

"The first time somebody knocked you down, you'd start bawling."

"Would not!"

"Would too!"

Mom places a steaming bowl in the centre of the table. "That's enough, both of you."

"I hate green beans!" Courtney whines and waves her fork. "You always make Jessie's favourite foods! You never make mine!"

Mom sighs and drops a spoonful of vegetables onto Courtney's plate. "Can you just be quiet until we're done talking about this?"

Courtney hangs her head and pouts, then noisily scrapes the green beans away from her mashed potatoes.

"Jessie doesn't know the first thing about hockey." Dad points at me with his steak knife. "She can't learn the game overnight."

Mom sits down in her seat and glares at him. "You're not making this any easier."

We all sit in awkward silence for a while.

"Mom, where did you get the idea of signing me up for hockey?" I can't contain my curiosity. "I never even knew there was girls' hockey here until Tara Brewer told me."

Mom takes a sip of water before continuing. "It was Constable Brewer's idea."

"You already told me about cleaning up Lignite. When did girls' hockey come up?" I push my plate to one side.

"He asked what activities you were involved in last year. When I mentioned ringette, he told me about his daughter's hockey team. He's the coach. Did you know that?"

I am beginning to feel trapped.

"They need players. And you skate very well. Don't you think you could at least give it a try — maybe go to practice tomorrow and see if you like it? Steve does seem very nice."

"Yeah, he's nice," I agree. "But I'm not going to that practice."

"I don't know," Dad says. "It seems kind of late for her to start hockey."

Mom shoots Dad a killing look, then places a hand on my forearm. "Are you afraid to give this a try?"

"I'm not afraid," I say. Afraid is what I felt facing Marsha. Still, my stomach feels uneasy when I think about learning how to shoot a puck — in front of Kim's friends. And what about all those rules? I don't even know what icing is.

Mom persists. "You'll never really know if you don't like hockey until you try it."

"It's just like green eggs and ham," Courtney explains.

"More like green beans and ham." Mom gestures at the uneaten legumes on Courtney's plate. "But thanks for the help."

Dad raises an eyebrow. I can tell he is struggling to keep silent.

"I'm not afraid," I repeat. "I just don't like hockey. And I'm not going to the rink tomorrow — no way."

"We'll see about that," Mom says.

chapter five

Mom and I arrive at the rink forty-five minutes before practice on Sunday afternoon.

"You do this," Mom says, "and maybe we'll forget to charge you for the liquor."

I am already dressed in my ringette equipment and the hockey pants, shin pads, and shoulder pads Mom borrowed from a neighbour's son. Yet another neighbour loaned her a stick. I hope it's the right length.

I made Dad and Courtney stay home, and Mom is under strict orders to leave as soon as she drops me off at the rink. It's bad enough to make a fool of myself, but doing it in front of my family is unthinkable.

As I climb out of the car and follow Mom across the parking lot, my hockey pants make this loud swishing noise. I feel like the Michelin Man. Some of the girls on my ringette team wore hockey equipment for extra protection, but I never did because I thought it would slow me down. Mom says I have to wear a mouthguard too. Great. When I talk to the girls on the ice, I'll sound retarded.

Mom stops in the middle of the lobby and drops the weathered bag containing my helmet, gloves and skates. "You promised to give this a fair shake." She darts a glance at the group of hockey moms standing by the Coke machine. "Behave yourself."

"Let's not forget about your end of the deal," I remind her, laying my hockey stick on top of the bag.

Mom nods.

No liquor bill – and Saskatoon to boot. A whole weekend with Tayja, Bailey and Keisha. It beats this by a mile.

A tall, slender woman with auburn hair approaches us, smiling broadly. "You must be Jessie. I'm Charlene Brewer, Tara's mom. I'm also the team manager."

Mom returns the smile and shakes Mrs. Brewer's hand. "I'm Diane McIntyre."

"Jessie, the team is in Dressing Room #1," Mrs. Brewer says. "I'll introduce you to the girls – although you must know a few of them already."

Mom picks up the sticks and equipment bag and hands them to me. "Are you sure you don't want me to come with you?"

I roll my eyes.

Mom gently pats my shoulder. "I'll see you after practice. Have fun."

Mrs. Brewer is already heading towards the double doors leading into the arena. "We're lucky to have you on the team, Jessie." She holds one of the doors open.

"I'm just here for one practice. I won't be back," I say quietly.

Her smile slips a fraction. "Well, hopefully you'll have so much fun you'll want to come back. Hockey can be addictive."

The loud report of a puck smacking the Plexiglas near my head startles me. A boys' minor hockey team is practising on the ice. I wonder how many years it would take me to develop a shot like that.

Mrs. Brewer leads me to a narrow passageway and approaches a grey door marked with a large number one. As soon as she opens the door, the stench of old sweat and the sound of young laughter drift out.

"I saw you slow dance with him at least three times, Tara." The girl who is speaking has shoulder-length blonde hair poking out from underneath a skater's toque. "You had your head on his shoulder the whole time."

"He's just a friend," Tara replies.

I can't see Tara as my view of the dressing room is blocked by the open door.

"Right. And my grandma got her belly button pierced."

"Your grandma got her belly button pierced?" another voice asks incredulously.

"Amber, you are such a ditz," someone moans.

"Girls, this is Jessie McIntyre." Mrs. Brewer moves aside so I can enter the room. The chatter and laughter fades. The girls, in various states of dress and undress, gaze at me inquisitively. Surveying the room, I recognize a few faces and am surprised to see so many welcoming smiles.

Tara, dressed only in a sports bra, spandex shorts, and shin pads, waves from her seat on the bench. "Good to see you, Jessie." She clears off a spot beside her. "Come sit next to me and I'll introduce you to the Xtreme. The only one missing today is Carla."

I sit down with a loud swish of my hockey pants. Too late I realize I am still holding my hockey stick. I must look like an idiot.

Shauna is seated across from me, tying her skates. When she straightens up, she holds up her hands as if she is driving a motorcycle and makes some Vroom-Vroom noises. At first I have no clue what she is doing. Then I remember. This isn't ringette.

Mrs. Brewer faces Tara. "Try not to be the last one out of the dressing room after practice. I have a hair appointment at 4:30."

After Mrs. Brewer exits, there's a moment's awkward pause. Then Tara begins introducing me to Miranda Ebberts, Kathy Parker — the girl in the toque — and Teneil

Howard, who are second-year Bantams, and Larissa Bilku, Jennifer McQueen and Amber Kowalski, who are first years.

"Kowalski?" I echo. "Are you related to the teacher Kowalski?"

Amber is slightly built and has the largest blue eyes I have ever seen. "He's my dad," she says.

I groan. "No offence, Amber, but he's —"

A sharp elbow jab from Tara stops me from completing my sentence.

"— my science teacher," I finish.

"I hate it that my dad's a teacher," Amber says bitterly. "Everybody tells me he's boring."

Tara laughs as she steps into her hockey pants. "You're just lucky your dad isn't a cop!"

Kathy yanks off her toque and rubs her scalp with her fingertips. "Hey, speaking of cops, did you guys hear about that stuff getting wrecked in Lignite on Halloween?"

Jennifer, a tall brunette with pale skin, says, "There was lots of damage in Lignite, but Mom says it was out-of-town kids, not locals."

"Jennifer's from Lignite," Tara tells me. "She played boys' hockey there until this year."

"I heard some kids got caught," volunteers Teneil, a freckle-faced girl with light brown hair.

Cheeks flaming, I dump my bag on the floor and begin to rummage through it for my skates.

Teneil continues. "I don't know who got picked up. Do you, Tara?"

"No! How many times do I have to tell you guys! Dad doesn't tell me anything!"

"How come you weren't at the dance, Jessie?" Teneil asks.

I give my standard reply. "I had to babysit."

"You gotta get out more, girl." Miranda, who has skin like milk chocolate and a gold ring through her black eyebrow, shoves her hand into her blocker. "Or you are going to dry up and blow away."

"You have to excuse Miranda for the way she talks," says Shauna. "She thinks she's black."

Everyone bursts into laughter, except Miranda who throws a roll of tape at Shauna's head.

"So, where's Carla?" asks Kathy when everyone has settled down.

"In Medicine Hat." Tara turns to me to explain. "Carla's older brother plays with the Tigers."

I have no idea who the Tigers are, but I figure Carla's brother must be a hockey player.

"Is Carla from Estevan?" I ask.

"Oxbow," Shauna declares.

"Larissa, will your dad be able to come to our away

49

games?" Tara asks the thin East Indian girl seated in the corner next to Amber.

Larissa shrugs. "He's going to try."

"Larissa's dad is Dr. Bilku," Tara says. "And my mom is a nurse. You'll never have to worry about getting looked after if you get hurt."

"Do people get hurt a lot?" I ask. "I thought girls' hockey was no contact."

"No body contact," Kathy says, smacking her chest with the heel of her hand. "But rubbing out along the boards is definitely allowed."

"Yes, rubbing out — not charging — not boarding — not checking-from-behind," Shauna responds, making the referee's signal for each infraction. She looks at me and jerks her head in Kathy's direction. "In case you hadn't guessed, Parker here is queen of the penalty box. She had more penalty minutes last year than the rest of us put together. It's something she's going to work on this year, right Parker?"

Kathy rolls her eyes and changes the subject. "Tara, did Mark have practice on Friday night?" She abruptly pulls on her helmet and flips up the visor.

Tara nods.

"His coach is a maniac!" Teneil cries. "Whoever heard of hockey practice on Halloween night?"

"It was an optional practice," Tara points out.

"Isn't 'optional' just another way of saying, 'If you don't show up, you're not dressing for the next game'?" asks Shauna.

"How'd you guys do at districts?" asks Miranda.

"We sucked," Shauna responds. "I hate playing volleyball against Weyburn and Midale."

"How did the ball-hog play?" Kathy asks in a teasing tone.

Before Shauna can reply, a brisk rapping on the door interrupts their conversation, which I am having great difficulty following. Near as I can figure, Mark is Tara's boyfriend, and he plays hockey too. I hope the ball-hog is Kim.

"Are you decent, girls?" comes a muffled voice from outside, a voice I recognize immediately.

Tara snatches her practice jersey and hauls it over her shoulder pads.

Kathy shouts, "No way! We're doing our traditional naked tribal dance around the garbage can!"

"What did you say?"

"I said — come on in, Coach!" Kathy laughs.

Constable Brewer, wearing skates, a black wind suit and a matching baseball cap, enters the room. A clipboard is tucked beneath his arm.

"Very funny. Is everyone here?" he asks.

"Everybody except Carla," Tara responds.

He points a large forefinger in my direction. "How're you doing, Jessie? Got everything you need?"

"I think so, Mr. Brewer."

The girls all start giggling for some reason.

"In here and on the ice, please call me Steve. I hope the girls have done their best to make you feel at home." Steve looks daggers at everyone, and they stop giggling.

I bob my head.

Steve glances briefly at his wristwatch. "Ten minutes until ice time. This is just a practice, but we have a game against Weyburn here on Tuesday night. Can everybody make it?"

"What time?" Shauna asks.

"Six thirty."

Kathy and Teneil high-five over top of Miranda. "I feel a hat trick coming on," Kathy crows. "Let's make Weyburn BLEED."

Steve aims a menacing finger at Kathy. "Weyburn has a strong team this year. Don't get cocky."

Kathy grins. "Aw, Coach, you tell us that every year."

"And Ebberts, for the last time, get that metal off your face."

Miranda reaches immediately for her eyebrow ring. "Right, Coach."

Next Steve turns his dark blue eyes on me, and I feel a little pang of fear. "Will you be able to make it on Tuesday? I know we're not giving you much time to get used to the game, but we need you."

I shrug, speechless.

"Let her decide after the practice, Dad," Tara says. "I think she's feeling overwhelmed."

"Let me know as soon as you can. If you can't make it, I'll have to call one of the Peewee girls."

"Get Randi Hilderman!" Kathy cries. "She'll set me up for that hat trick!"

Steve heads for the door. "Ice time, girls. And remember – if you skate hard in practice..."

"You'll skate hard in the game," Amber says.

The Xtreme – except for Tara and me – gather up sticks and gloves and begin filing out of the dressing room.

I wait until the other girls are gone, then ask the question that's been nagging me all weekend. "Why did you ask me to play hockey?"

Tara calmly goes on lacing her left skate. "We need players, Jessie. Hasn't everybody made that clear?" She doubles the knot and sits up straight. "Is there something else bothering you?"

I take a deep breath. "You and Kim Scott are friends – right?"

"Sort of. We've played on a few teams together. Why do you ask?"

"I don't get along with Kim."

"So I've heard." Tara stands and picks up her sticks. "But that has nothing to do with us. Kim's not on the Xtreme and probably never will be. She says girls' hockey sucks." Tara opens the dressing room door and stares at me for a minute. "Jessie, just relax. You look like a bundle of nerves. If you're worried about playing hockey and screwing up, you're wrong."

"What makes you so sure?"

"Teneil was a figure skater before she started playing with the Xtreme, and she's doing all right. Shauna and I wouldn't have asked you to play if we didn't think you could do it."

"Thanks."

What am I doing here, I wonder, after one lap around the rink. My shoulder pads are chafing, and the tape holding up my shin pads is cutting off the circulation in my right calf.

But after the second circuit, I have to admit how great it feels to be back on the ice.

I watch the other girls and try to imitate their movements. Shauna is by far the best skater. She has long, powerful strides that eat up the ice. Tara, Kathy and Jennifer look equal in ability while Teneil, Amber and Larissa lag a little behind.

Miranda, whose goalie pads hamper her speed, brings up the rear.

"Having some problems adjusting to the equipment?" Shauna calls to me as she leads the stretches at the red faceoff dot. The Xtreme are sprawled in a circle around her.

"Is it that obvious?" My face is burning with embarrassment.

"Hey, don't feel bad," she says quickly. "It took Teneil three months to get used to hockey skates."

Kathy says to me. "You're an awesome skater. Sometime I wanna hear more about this ringette you used to play."

In spite of my suspicions, a pleasurable glow ignites in my belly. I can't help it. The girls are all just too nice. "Sure."

"You're gonna fit in just fine, girl," Miranda says and begins singing "Superstar" in her low, slightly off-key voice, and the rest of the girls join in.

After a few minutes, I ask Tara, "Do you play many games?"

"We played twenty-nine last year. Tuesday's will be our first." Tara leans over and nearly touches her nose to the ice.

I'd love to be that flexible.

"We don't belong to a league. Mom just arranges games for us. There are more girls' teams this year, so hopefully we won't have to play the Peewee boys' teams very often."

"You play against boys?" My heart sinks to the pit of my stomach.

"Yes," Tara says, "and we usually beat them."

By now the girls have stopped singing and are listening intently to our conversation.

Miranda sighs. "Once we lost to my brother's team, and he never let me hear the end of it. There's nothing worse than being scored on by your own brother."

"What about getting beaten by a kid you used to baby-sit?" Kathy asks.

Steve blows his whistle, and Shauna immediately skates towards the players' box, where Steve and another man are waiting. Most of the girls follow.

"What now?" I awkwardly get to my feet, still cursing the pants.

"Just a little power skating," Tara says.

Steve's companion, a slightly built man with a receding hairline, looks very familiar. "Is that Mr. Kowalski?" I ask.

"Yep, he's our trainer. He also helps Dad run practices and coach. He'll be working with you today."

Great.

"So, how was practice?" Mom asks as I heave my equipment bag into the back of the Explorer.

"Okay." I climb into the passenger seat and shut the door. "Can I get something to drink?"

"Do you want to stop at 7-Eleven and get a juice or something?"

"All right." I fasten my seat belt.

"Do you think you'll want to go back?" Mom turns to face me. "I think it's very important that you give this hockey thing a decent shot – pardon the pun."

I nod. "It wasn't what I expected."

"What do you mean?"

"I expected it to be hard – and it was. But it was fun too. I spent most of the practice with Mr. Kowalski, working on giving and taking passes. "

"Just back up a second," Mom says. "Did you say Mr. Kowalski?"

"Yeah, my science teacher. His daughter's on the team."

Mom leans her head back as far as her seat will allow and stares at the roof. "And how did you get along with him – or dare I ask?"

"Great, actually. He says next practice he'll help me with carrying the puck and taking wrist shots."

On the way home, I describe each of the girls on the team, as well as the drills. Looking at Mom's smiling profile as we turn down our street, I can tell she is thrilled. Frankly, I'm pretty excited too.

"So the girls were nice to you?"

"They were great, Mom – especially Tara and Shauna.

Oh, and one more thing," I add as we pull into the driveway. "Our first game is on Tuesday. Steve wants me to play. Do you think I can go – even though I'm grounded?"

Mom looks surprised. "Do you think you're ready to play a game?"

I laugh out loud. "No! But Steve promised I could just watch the first period – and then he'd let me play a few shifts so I could get used to it. Can I go, Mom? Please?"

Mom grins. "Only if you'll let me watch."

chapter six

t school on Monday morning, the students are buzzing with the usual gossip. As I walk down the Grade Nine hallway, I feel the stares and whispers like a second skin.

Crap. Everybody knows about Halloween.

I go straight to my locker and, opening it quickly, check my schedule. Language Arts with Mr. Wallis. Good start. I begin searching my shelves for my binder and anthology.

"Since when did you start playing girls' hockey?" a voice behind me asks.

With shaking hands, I pull my books out of my locker and slam the door. I turn and find myself face to face with Kim Scott, Natalie Wilgenbush and a handful of other girls from my homeroom.

"Since Sunday," I reply firmly. I can't stop myself from adding, "What's it to you?"

Kim raises an eyebrow. "Hockey isn't one bit like ringette,

you know. It's much harder to carry a puck on your stick than a little rubber ring." She takes a step backwards and exchanges smirks with Natalie. "Of course, girls' hockey is a joke anyway."

"You should fit right in with those wannabes," Natalie says.

"So that makes Shauna and Tara wannabes?" I ask.

I am not surprised when Kim changes the subject.

"Hear you did some partying in Lignite on Halloween night." She leans in so that our faces are only inches apart. We are more or less the same height, so I am looking right into her cool, green eyes. "Find time to do some trick-or-treating?"

A crowd has started to gather around us. Simply great.

"It's none of your business," I say quietly.

Kim leans over and says right in my ear. "Heard you got picked up by the RCs. Spent the night in the slammer with some drunks."

Natalie adds triumphantly, "Ever wonder why Marsha thought you were spreading rumors about her?"

I stare at both of them, speechless. It's hard to believe they would stoop that low.

"Didn't the two of you hit it off?" Kim asks. "I thought you needed a friend."

The smug look she is wearing pushes me over the edge. I throw down my books and launch myself at her, knocking her to the floor. The crowd surrounding us hums with excitement.

"Chick fight!" a male voice yells.

Without the slightest hesitation, Kim leaps to her feet and rams her shoulder into my chest, throwing me against the lockers. I grab a handful of her hair, but she punches me in the face twice, and my nose starts bleeding. She wrestles me to the ground and sits on my chest, grabbing my jaw with one hand and pinning my arms beneath her knees. Humiliated, I try to squirm out from underneath her.

"Had enough?" she demands.

Choking on the blood that is now running down the back of my throat, I cough and sputter, spraying her white Roots t-shirt. She keeps squeezing my face. I can't believe that no one tries to stop her. Natalie and the others are laughing and pointing.

"What's going on out here?" Mr. Wallis' stern voice shouts.

Kim abruptly releases my chin, and my head bangs the floor. When I open my eyes, I see Tara's and Shauna's shocked faces looking down at me.

Mr. Wallis pushes through the crowd of students. "Kim, get off that girl! Jessie, are you hurt?"

Kim does as she's told. I shake my head dizzily and begin to sit up. My pride is injured worse than anything else.

Suddenly, Tara's voice is in my ear. "Here, let me help you."

My first instinct is to refuse, but my knees are shaking so bad they'll never support me. Embarrassed, I let Tara pull me to my feet and put her arm around me.

Nearly a hundred students use this part of the hallway, and I'm sure every one of them is staring at me. I refuse to look at Kim or Natalie.

"Kim, come with me." Mr. Wallis takes charge. "Tara, take Jessie to the washroom so she can wash her face, then bring her to the office." He claps his hands loudly. "The rest of you get to your homerooms! Move it!"

The crowd parts for us as we walk down the hallway. Tara's wiry arm is wrapped around my waist. I cup my hand under my chin but still manage to drip blood all the way to the girls' washroom.

Once we are alone, Tara asks incredulously, "What happened out there?"

I feel a surge of anger. Some teammate. She and Shauna did nothing to stop Kim. I grab a handful of paper towel and douse it with cold water, then put a plug in my nose to soak up the blood. Kim's fingertips are imprinted in red on both my cheeks, and my eye is already starting to swell shut. Fortunately, my black T-shirt doesn't show the red stains, but there are plenty of spots on my jeans and runners.

Tara persists. "Jessie, why did Kim pin you down?"

I wipe my eyes with the paper towel and stare at Tara's reflection in the mirror over the sink.

"Kim's tough as hell. Did you really think you were going to win a fight with her?" Tara leans against the counter beside me. "She also carries a grudge for a long, long time. Your little scrap with her today isn't going to make things any better."

"Don't you think I know that?" I angrily slam the wad of paper towel in the wastebasket and pull another piece off the dispenser. "I hate her guts! And if you knew what she did to me, you'd hate her too!"

Tara leans her hip against the countertop. "I know she doesn't like you very much. Did you say something to piss her off?"

I remove the plug and splash my face with a few handfuls of water. I dry it off before replying. "Why didn't you and Shauna help me out there? Instead of just standing and watching?" My lower lip begins to quiver. I can't help it.

That shocks Tara into silence.

By now I am sobbing. "I thought you were my friends!"

Tara's dark blue eyes grow wide. "We were all the way down the hall when it started! We came as fast as we could!"

I wipe my eyes and look at myself in the mirror. I am in no condition to leave the washroom.

Tara puts her arms around me. "By the time we got there, Mr. Wallis was already breaking it up. I'm sorry we didn't get there sooner."

I sob into her shoulder for a long time, and she doesn't even seem to mind that I'm getting blood and snot and tears all over her shirt. She keeps rubbing my back and telling me it's going to be okay. I wish I could believe her.

Kim and I spend the rest of the day on an in-school suspension. I also get a one-day out-of-school while Kim gets two for punching me. Mom and Dad are both at the school by ten o'clock and meet with Mrs. Wright, the principal, in her office. Eventually, I have to go in and talk to them too. Mom starts to cry when she sees my face, so I know I must look terrible. I say nothing the whole time because it seems to be the easiest way. After a while Mrs. Wright gives up and sends me to the detention room, where Kim and I spend an uncomfortable morning sniping at one another. The teacher assistant in charge tries to referee, but she doesn't have much luck getting us to do any school work.

A short, aggressive-looking woman who must be Kim's mom shows up before lunch and throws a tantrum in Mrs. Wright's office. In the end, Mrs. Wright says she will reconsider the punishment if Kim and I apologize to one another or at least agree to peer mediation. Both of us refuse. Then Mrs. Scott drags Kim out the door, making threats and accusations.

"One of the board members is a very good friend of mine!" she shouts. "Believe me, this is not going to end here! You owe my daughter an apology, and she's going to get it!"

What Mrs. Wright has to apologize for, I can't imagine.

By the time Mom returns to pick me up, it's four o'clock. As we walk out of the school, I can't bring myself to look Mom in the eye or say a word. Mom, on the other hand, has plenty to say.

"I just don't understand," she says. "What's going on between you and this other girl?"

"Nothing."

Mom nearly explodes. "You call a suspension from school nothing? I am so embarrassed, I don't know what to say!"

I kick a pebble down the sidewalk.

Mom opens the driver's door on the Explorer. "I really thought — I really hoped — you hit rock bottom last weekend, but I was wrong. It's going to be one thing after another, isn't it?"

I slide into the passenger seat and open the console, looking for the bottle of Tylenol Mom keeps there. My temples are throbbing. When I look in the mirror on the back of the sun visor, I discover that my left eye has turned black. I look like a prizefighter that stayed up for too many rounds.

Mom pounds the steering wheel with her fist. "What am I going to tell your grandparents?"

I open my mouth to say that I don't care, but the words die on my lips. Marsha and another girl are leaning against the metal railing that surrounds the school grounds. A rusty old sedan with the paint peeling off the roof is parked at the curb.

Like a pair of stray dogs who have caught my scent, the girls straighten and glare at me as we drive by. For a moment, my eyes meet Marsha's, and the hair prickles on the back of my neck.

"Who are you looking at?" Mom asks.

"Nobody." I watch them in the side mirror until we turn at the corner and they are lost from sight. "Mom, when you pick up Courtney for figure skating tomorrow, will you pick me up too?"

"It's nice that you're taking an interest in your sister, considering that you abandoned her on the weekend." Mom digs in her purse for her cellphone. "Call your father and tell him we've left the school. He wants to talk to you."

Another lecture. Great.

Marsha may be gone from view – but not from memory. "Do you think I could go to Saskatoon this weekend? I could take the bus and stay with Bailey."

"You have community service, remember?" Mom says tartly. She pauses for a moment, and then adds in a different tone, "You can tell your dad that I think you should play that game on Tuesday night. We were discussing it earlier."

"Really?"

"The team seems to be a positive influence on you. After practice on Sunday, you looked happy for the first time in months."

I think about the way Tara tried to comfort me in the washroom. And her promise that she and Shauna would try to protect me from Kim. Would they be able to do the same with Marsha and her friends?

"Will Dad drive me to the rink and stay for the entire game?" I ask.

"Of course. He's dying to see you on the ice."

I start punching in his work number on the phone. "You know, Mom, if I had a cellphone of my own..."

Mom stares straight ahead. "Don't even think about it."

chapter
seven

n Tuesday afternoon when I walk into the Xtreme's dressing room, a host of watchful expressions greets me. It's obvious that the girls know about my arrest on the weekend and suspension from school. They probably think I'm a real loser.

Shauna's the first to break the silence. "Hey, Jessie. Ready to play your first game of hockey?"

"Not really." I laugh nervously. I drop my equipment bag in the corner and hang my jacket on a hook. I'm dressing with the team tonight.

"Well, you sure *look* like a hockey player," Kathy says, smothering a laugh. "Nice shiner!"

"Carla isn't back from the Hat, so Dad asked Randi Hilderman to play." Tara gestures to an athletic-looking girl with long red hair who is sitting next to her. "Randi – this is Jessie."

I nod at the younger girl, and reaching into my hockey bag, remove an old T-shirt and boxer shorts.

"We heard you were involved with that vandalism on Halloween night," Shauna says.

I straighten and face Shauna, clutching the clothing against my chest. My heart is hammering.

"We'd like to hear your side of the story."

"Why is it any of your business?" I ask.

Shauna runs a slender hand through her blonde hair. "Whatever you do reflects on all of us."

I knew this was coming, but I am still not prepared to explain. How can I tell them what Kim has been doing? How she set me up to be beaten to a pulp by Marsha? They've known Kim for years, and I'm just the new kid. "It won't happen again," I say simply. "That's all you need to know."

Shauna and Tara exchange concerned looks.

"If you say so," Shauna says at last.

"Well, Kim's got issues with you — that's for sure." Kathy scratches her head through her toque. "She's mentioned you the odd time on MSN."

"The odd time?" Miranda asks in a significant tone.

Tara nods. "Maybe it would be a good idea to steer clear of her from now on."

"It's hard to avoid her — seeing as how she's in my home-room," I counter.

"Just the same — you should try to take Tara's advice." Shauna surveys the room. "And we also need to know if we can depend on you to show up for games and practices."

"I'm doing my best, okay?" I plead.

"That's good enough for me," Miranda says brightly. "Now let's all lighten up a little. Kathy wants to tell Jessie and Randi about the time she lowered the shoulder on Weyburn's captain."

I listen with only half an ear as Kathy gives a detailed and probably exaggerated account of the incident, actively role-playing the parts of both players. I keep glancing at Shauna and Tara, but they are too busy talking to Jennifer about a hockey school the three of them attended last August.

Mrs. Brewer walks into the dressing room, carrying an armload of black-white-and-gold jerseys.

"Sorry I don't have matching socks for all of you," she says. "I see that some of you have been hoarding yours from last year." She pauses to take note of the girls already wearing black socks with wide gold and narrow white stripes. "Veterans get the same number as last year. Is that all right?"

She begins calling out numbers, and the girls obediently take their jerseys from her. They look just like the ones worn by the Boston Bruins, except that there's an E instead of a B at the center of the logo. Kathy is obviously very proud of the number 10 she wears with the A sewn on the left shoulder. Tara, wearing number 17, is also an assistant captain. I am not surprised to see Shauna pull on the number 4 jersey, which bears a C.

"Jessie, you'll wear number 13." Mrs. Brewer hands me the last jersey. "I hope this will be a lucky number for you."

I'd prefer to wear 14, my number on the Stars, but that's Teneil's number. I pull the jersey over my head and shoulders. "Does it look all right?"

Mrs. Brewer smiles. "It looks great."

I stare ruefully at my green-navy-and-white socks, which I snitched from my dad's hockey bag. "The socks clash."

"Should look great with that blue helmet too," says Jennifer.

Is she making fun of me? I shoot her a look, but she's smiling in a friendly way, so I don't take offence.

"I'll get you matching socks as soon as I can. Good luck to you girls." Mrs. Brewer gathers up the hangers. "And remember to have fun."

"Oh, we always have fun, Mom. You know that!" Tara grins.

Mrs. Brewer faces her daughter, hands on her broad hips. "Tara, get your equipment on, will you? The coaches will be here any minute!"

If Mr. Kowalski knows anything about my arrest or the fight with Kim, he doesn't give any indication. He and Steve are totally preoccupied with the task of making up the lines and giving last minute instructions. The Xtreme take all of this in stride, obviously used to a barrage of advice, but my head is positively reeling with the effort to remember everything. I think I know what Steve means about "not giving the opposition the middle of the ice," but he keeps talking about "supporting the puck" and "the rink inside the rink." What does all that mean?

It occurs to me that Steve might just be the most technical coach I've ever known. With his help, maybe I'll be able to contribute something to this team.

For the past week, Dad has been quizzing me every night about the differences between ringette and hockey — like offsides and icings — but I now find myself worrying about simpler things. Where should I stand when I line up for a faceoff? I don't even know what position I'm playing.

Watching the Weyburn Red Wings warm up, I am amazed that Kathy is so confident we'll win. The Red Wings seem bigger, and they can certainly skate as well as any of us.

Moments later, when the Weyburn coaches toss out the pucks, I figure it out. Though able to skate well, the Red Wings don't have one player who can stickhandle like Tara or Shauna.

The horn goes off to indicate that the teams should line up for the opening faceoff, and I skate to the box.

Mr. Kowalski, who is running the forwards, pats me on the shoulder. "Are you nervous?"

I nod, my stomach turning somersaults at the thought of stepping back on the ice.

"You'll play right wing since you shoot right. That'll make it easier for you to give and take passes."

I look over at Tara and Larissa, my linemates. I wish I could look that relaxed. Randi is talking to Steve, who runs the defence. At centre ice, Kathy lines up with her two wingers, Teneil and Amber, while Shauna and Jennifer take up the defensive positions behind them. Looking around the arena, I don't see many spectators, just a handful of parents and siblings, including my dad. I know Mom and Courtney will be watching from the indoor gallery above the north end of the rink.

A moment later the referee drops the puck, and the game is underway. Kathy easily wins the faceoff and passes to Teneil, who puts a move on the Weyburn right winger and goes wide down the ice. At the right moment, she passes back to Kathy in the slot, but Kathy isn't able to hang on. A Weyburn defenceman rips the puck around the boards and out of her end.

"Nice pass, Teneil!" Larissa screams through her mouth-guard. At least that's what I think she said.

"Kathy's a little rusty," Tara says. "She doesn't usually miss a nice one like that."

Looking up, I see that the three Weyburn forwards are now bearing down on Shauna. The Weyburn captain neatly pushes the puck through Shauna's skates and slides around her, creating a 3 on 0 on Miranda. For a second, it looks like the captain will pass the puck, but instead she takes a hard wrist shot going top right corner. Miranda snatches the puck out of the air and stares down the three Weyburn players as the referee blows the whistle to announce a faceoff in our end.

"Let's go." Tara gives me a little push towards the door, which Mr. Kowalski holds open.

"So soon?" Terrified, I stare at the clock.

Not even a minute has elapsed.

"Dad likes short shifts," Tara explains.

I turn to Mr. Kowalski in desperation. "I thought I was just going to watch for the first period!"

"We only have six forwards, Jessie. It's baptism by fire."

More like baptism by drowning. I step onto the ice, my legs trembling and my insides spinning like clothes in a dryer.

Tara and Larissa help me find my position at the faceoff dot next to the tallest player on the Weyburn team. She is wearing number 44.

"It's my first game," I say.

"You're a fat cow," she replies.

That's nice!

When the puck drops, she elbows me in the head and hooks my skates out from under me.

Sitting on my butt, I have a perfect view as she receives a pass from the Weyburn centre and slides the puck between

Miranda's legs. Maybe these Weyburn girls are better than I thought. Shauna skates over to Miranda and taps her pads in consolation, then tosses the puck to the linesman.

"Don't worry about it." Tara pats me on the back as we skate to centre ice.

"That girl elbowed me in the head – and she tripped me too!" I angrily point at Number 44 with the blade of my stick. "Shouldn't she get a penalty?"

"Most of our refs don't call penalties," Tara explains. "And if they do, they call far too many. Get used to it."

Next faceoff, I manage to keep my feet. Tara wins the draw and passes to Larissa, who easily catches the puck on the back of her blade. I am nearly at the blue line when Larissa's backhanded shot sails into the net over the Weyburn goaltender's right shoulder. A little celebration takes place in front of the crease as Tara, Shauna and Jennifer smack Larissa's helmet and cheer her all the way back to the Xtreme bench with me trailing behind.

"Well, your plus-minus is now zero, Jessie," Mr. Kowalski comments as we line up along the boards.

"Her what is what?" Amber asks, puzzled.

That makes me feel a little better. Even I know that a player gets a minus if she's on the ice for an opposition goal, and a plus if she's on when her team scores. Dad is always saying that his hero Bobby Orr is the all time leader in plus-minuses.

I watch Kathy's line score another goal. Maybe Kathy was right after all. She certainly isn't having any trouble scoring on Weyburn.

Mr. Kowalski says we have the ice for only one and a half hours. We'll play two twenty-five-minute periods of straight time, flood the ice, and play a final stop time period of twenty minutes.

"Isn't a period normally twenty minutes of stop time?" I ask.

"Ice time is a precious commodity around here," Mr. Kowalski replies. "Take your complaints to the rec board."

I have at least a dozen shifts in the first period. After five, I have a nagging stitch in my side, my lungs are burning, and my legs are shaking so badly I have to sit down when I'm not skating. I have been rubbed out against the boards six times, and my forearms are bruised from the slashing penalty Number 16 took. I can't remember successfully clearing the puck out of our zone much less catching a pass.

In spite of all this, I am having the time of my life. Whenever I make a mistake, the girls tease me for a while and then give me loads of advice and encouragement. I don't know why I was so afraid to try something new.

My line's most memorable moment occurs when Tara lines up at the faceoff dot across from the Weyburn captain, and their helmets somehow get hooked. Or course Larissa and I don't even notice, and we break down the ice. When we hear the ref's whistle, we turn around and see the two girls, who look pretty much like a pair of deer with their antlers caught. Larissa starts howling, and so do I. Pretty soon, both teams are in stitches.

With each shift I am gaining more confidence.

"You have a natural aggressiveness, Jessie, and you're a terrific skater." Mr. Kowalski pats me on top of the helmet. "You must have been one heck of a ringette player."

I am definitely going to start getting better marks in his science class.

Although we have a stronger offence, the Red Wings' defence prevents us from scoring again until the end of the first period. Shauna scores our third goal unassisted by bringing the puck all the way down the ice from behind our own net.

"You won't see Shauna rush very often," Mr. Kowalski observes as Randi grabs Shauna around the waist and tries to lift her up. "She's one fine stay-at-home defenceman."

"Has Shauna been playing hockey long?"

"Since she was old enough to walk. She played boys' hockey until last year, even played on a Tier 1 team for a season."

"How come she started playing with the girls?"

"Her older brother had a serious concussion a few years

ago — his third one — and hasn't played hockey since. Her parents didn't want the same thing to happen to her, not when she loves the sport so much."

"Do the girls' teams ever get really rough — I mean, rougher than Weyburn?" I ask, thinking about Number 44.

"Oh, yeah," says Tara. "Wait till we play the Notre Dame Hounds."

The horn blows, ending the first period.

We are allowed a five-minute break to regroup and switch ends. Steve asks me how I'm doing.

"Good, Coach." I feel a little self-conscious because the Xtreme are all staring at me. "I just wish I was doing something to help the team. I've hardly touched the puck."

"Neither has the Weyburn goalie!" Kathy cackles. "Everything we shoot at her goes in!"

"Parker, stifle your enthusiasm. There's still lots of time left on the clock." Turning back to me, Steve adds, "And don't think you're not helping the team, Jessie. How are your legs holding up?"

"Okay," I lie.

"Just say the word if you need a longer rest. Some of these girls can double shift if they have to. Anyone think they're not getting enough ice time?"

A chorus of groans greets this remark. I am relieved to hear I'm not the only one with legs like cement.

"I'm sorry I can't catch a pass," I say to Tara as we sit down on the bench.

"Quit being so hard on yourself! You haven't gone offside once so far — and that's the hardest thing for most new players to learn. You should have seen Teneil last year."

I shake my head. "I'm crappy with the puck. I just can't seem to find the end of my stick."

Tara smacks my helmet. "You'll find it, I promise. Next shift, break down the ice, and I'll throw you a pass. Then you'll know you're in the game."

Tara is as good as her word. When the referee releases the puck to start the second period, I take off down the right wing, looking over my left shoulder for Tara's pass. It comes — right on the tape — but I can't hang on to it. I chase the puck into the corner, only to be rubbed out against the boards by good old Number 44. I get up just as Tara intercepts 44's pass attempt and shoots the puck back into my corner. This time I get to the puck first and find Tara in the slot. I fan on the shot just as 44's elbow connects with my head — again. I take another determined swipe at the puck and manage to throw it out in front of the crease. Tara one-times my pass right into the net.

In a moment, Larissa is hanging around my neck, and Tara is pounding my back. Jennifer and Randi complete the circle.

"Great pass!" Jennifer roars.

"Awesome!" Tara is saying. "You got your first assist, Jessie!"

When we line up again at centre ice, I have eyes for no one but 44. "Not bad for a rookie, huh?" I ask, my head still ringing from the blow.

The Weyburn defenceman shrugs. "Tell your boyfriend he was good last night."

I am speechless.

The puck drops, and play resumes.

I know one thing. Ringette was never like this.

We win the game 9-6. Afterward I am so tired that I just skate to the gate at the end of the arena and wait for someone to let me out. When it swings open, I find myself facing three boys wearing identical black windbreakers with a Bruin symbol on the chest. The tallest one has shoulder-length dark blond hair, a gold earring in his left ear, and the most amazing grey eyes.

He grabs Tara as she walks by and puts her in a headlock. "Whew, you stink!" he says.

Tara takes a swipe at his head with her hockey stick. "So do you!"

"You're crazy!" He holds up his arms to protect his face.

The other two boys start laughing, and then Shauna stops to talk to them too. I'd sure like to know who that guy with the earring is.

"Move it along, will ya!" comes Kathy's voice from behind. "Some of us need a shower!"

Reluctantly, I start walking toward the dressing room and leave Tara and Shauna behind. My parents and Courtney are waiting for me in the concourse.

"Great game, hon!" Mom squeezes my shoulder, then instinctively covers her nose. "I forgot about the smell!"

Dad laughs. "You looked like you were having fun out there, Jessie. Terrific game."

Courtney grabs my stick and hefts it experimentally. "When can I start playing hockey?" she asks.

Once inside the dressing room, I sit down next to Kathy, unable to contain my curiosity. "Who were those guys talking to Tara and Shauna?"

"Mark Taylor, Brian Smoltz and Nathan Reynolds. They all play with the Midget AA team." Kathy tears away a Velcro strap and drops her elbow pad on the floor.

"Were they watching us?" I ask, embarrassed.

Kathy shrugs. "They came to lots of our games last year. They're probably our best fans. Brian goes out with Shauna, and Mark and Tara are —"

"Hey, Jessie!" Mrs. Brewer enters the dressing room. "Are you coming to practice on Saturday? We also might have a game against a Peewee boys' team on Sunday night. Will you make it to both?"

"I can't come on Saturday," I reply, remembering my date with community service.

Mrs. Brewer nods. "What about Sunday?"

"I'll be there."

I'd like to sit back and enjoy the banter of the girls, but I want to get in and out of the shower before the rest of them. The whole team nudity thing makes me uneasy – although it doesn't seem to bother anybody else. I hastily strip down and wrap myself in a towel. When I head for the shower room, Kathy darts past me, still wearing her sports bra and boxers.

"Whoa!" she calls out. "Wait a minute, Jessie!"

"What?' I stare at her in confusion.

Kathy goes to the other end of the shower room and yells, "Don't come in! We're showering!"

A deep male voice replies, "Okay!"

Kathy hustles back towards me. "Now you can go."

I'm confused. "Who were you talking to?"

"The men's rec team in the other dressing room," she explains. "Did you really want them to walk in on you?" She raises an eyebrow significantly.

"Is it safe?" I stare into the empty shower room, all too aware of the male voices and laughter drifting over from the other side.

"Safe's for softball." Kathy gives me a little push. "Welcome to hockey!"

chapter
eight

n Thursday when Kim returns to school, I make a point of avoiding her and Natalie. Mr. Wallis has changed the seating plan in homeroom and in English class, so we sit nowhere near one another. I put on makeup to cover the bruises on my face, but I'm sure everybody can still see them. Whenever our eyes meet, Kim looks like she's planning my murder. I heard her tell the other girls that her mom complained to the director of the school division about the two-day suspension. As far as Mrs. Scott is concerned, I started the whole thing by knocking Kim down. Mrs. Scott would go ballistic if she knew how good that felt – well, for a second anyway.

"I hear you have a game on Sunday night," Kim says to me in the hallway between first and second class. "Maybe I'll come watch. I haven't had a good laugh since Monday."

Shortly after math class begins, Mrs. Graham says that the principal wants to see me. It's a relief to get out of the classroom for a while, even if it means getting grilled by Mrs. Wright and possibly stirring the pot even more than it's already stirred.

When I'm seated in her office, Mrs. Wright stretches out her long legs and asks, "What do you think about changing homerooms?"

Her question takes me by surprise. "What homeroom would you move me to?" I fold my arms across my chest and tuck my feet under the chair, trying to look casual.

"Because of scheduling, 217 is the only option. Mr. Kowalski would be your homeroom teacher."

217? Tara and Shauna's homeroom! Finally, things are going my way! "I really like Mr. Kowalski."

She gives me a piercing look. "So you wouldn't have any objections?"

I shake my head.

"I'll have to check with your parents first, but if they agree, you can start classes with 217 tomorrow morning. Mr. Kowalski will assign you a new locker." She stands up and leans against the window, where frost has created lacy patterns on the pane. "If you and Kim won't resolve your differences, you should at least avoid one another. Is that understood?"

I nod. What does she think I've been trying to do for the past two months?

"In the meantime, there are things you can do about harassment."

I stare at her in amazement. I've never told anyone about Kim's bullying. How does she know?

"You're not the first girl Kim has picked on, and you probably won't be the last. If you're blaming yourself for what's been going on, don't. She probably sees you as a threat and a rival."

A threat? Me?

"You got a great deal of attention when you arrived. She didn't like it. Underneath that tough, confident exterior, she's very insecure."

Kim – insecure? No way!

"I wish you'd told me what was going on. If I'd known, the suspensions would've been handled differently."

My point exactly. It was bad enough that I got one day less out-of-school than Kim did. She'll never forgive me for that.

"If you have a few minutes, I can tell you about some strategies to use with Kim – or other girls that bully you. Are you interested?"

I shrug my shoulders. "It can't hurt."

After school, I ask Mr. Wallis if I can clean out my locker and move my things to the new one down the hall.

He looks at me keenly for a moment. "Do you really think a change of homerooms is going to help?"

I'd like to tell Mr. Wallis that he needs to open his eyes and take a good look at Kim Scott and Natalie Wilgenbush, but I don't. Mrs. Wright told me this morning that male teachers are often blind to the behaviour of girls like Kim. "I hope it will," I say quietly, removing my lock and handing it to him. "Mr. Kowalski gave me a new lock. Kim knows the combination to this one."

He raises an eyebrow at this revelation. "I was talking to Mr. Kowalski in the staff room today." He leans against the next locker while I begin pulling out my texts and binders. "He said your attitude has greatly improved in science class. He also said you have lots of potential as a hockey player. Are you beginning to find out that Mr. Kowalski isn't so bad after all?"

"Let's just say he knows a lot more about hockey than he does about science."

Mr. Wallis smiles woodenly. "I was glad to hear that you've made some friends on the team. I think you're on the right track for the first time since you moved here, Jessie. Good luck, and let me know if you ever need my help."

He disappears into his classroom.

While I move my stuff from one locker to the other, I think about the advice Mrs. Wright gave me in her office. It feels good to know that I've already done some of the right things by blocking the girls on MSN and not responding to their emails. She also showed me some cool techniques on how to maintain my personal space and distract a bully by agreeing with her or changing the subject. I think her ideas might work on Kim — but I don't know about Marsha. Hopefully I've seen the last of her.

In twenty minutes, I've set up housekeeping in my new locker, which is at the other end of the hall. Just as I'm closing the door, I hear footsteps on the stairs, and the tall boy with the earring and black windbreaker turns the corner. The tempo of my heart accelerates immediately.

"Hi!" he says in a friendly tone. "Have you seen Tara Brewer?"

I shake my head and look away, afraid he'll see my bruises. "I think she left."

He takes off his baseball cap and scratches his head. "I was supposed to pick her up after school today. I wonder where she went."

"No idea." I wish I could think of some way to prolong this conversation.

"Well, thanks anyway." He starts to walk away.

"I play hockey with Tara." Honestly, it just blurts out of my mouth. Just like I spit on him or something.

He turns around. "You must be one of the new girls on the team. What's your name?"

"Jessie McIntyre."

"I'm Mark Taylor. Nice to meet you, Jessie."

I know I'm blushing. I hastily throw on my jacket, then pick up my math binder and textbook. I attach my lock with shaking hands. "It was my first hockey game – ever." I sneak a glance at him.

He looks impressed. "Wow. You did well then. Tara says you played ringette before you came here."

She's told him about me?

"Well, I gotta run. If Tara's not here, I better find out where she is."

When he starts back down the stairs, I follow him – just like a stupid groupie. "We have a game on Sunday night," I say.

"So I hear – against one of the Peewee boys' teams," he replies.

"Will you be coming?" I should kick myself a couple of times for being so obvious.

"I've got a doubleheader in Swift Current this weekend, so I'll have to miss. I play with the midget team, in case you didn't know."

He doesn't even say the AA Midgets. What a modest guy.

"I'd rather watch the Xtreme play a girls' team anyway," he adds.

"How come?" I realize I've been holding my breath.

By now we are at the bottom of the stairs and heading toward the main entrance.

"Girls' hockey is very different from the guy's game," he says, stopping at the door. "The girls may not be as skilled as the guys, but the game is still fast paced. And girls don't get in fights as often. They just swear and call each other names. I know – because I've reffed a few of Tara's games."

"Do you plan to ref any this year?"

He shakes his head. "Too busy. We're on the road lots." He pauses and adds, "You know – I think Tara's good enough to play on one of the elite Bantam boys' teams, but she has way more fun playing with you girls. Especially now that Shauna and Carla are on the team. She really likes you too."

I feel like crap all of a sudden. Here I am trying to keep up a conversation with him, and the whole time I'm forgetting he's Tara's guy. I don't deserve to have her for a friend. Better cut this off quick.

But as we step into the frigid November air, I notice half a dozen figures, who look too large to be junior high students, hanging around the bicycle rack at the end of the parking lot.

"Who's that?" asks Mark. "They look like they're up to something."

As we draw closer, I can pick out Marsha's stocky frame. Great. The boy with the backwards baseball cap has got to be Tyler. A pimped-out Camaro is parked next to the rack, which means Rick is there too.

I really am stupid for thinking I can put off a confronta-
tion with Marsha forever.

She's leaning against my mountain bike, which is the only
one left in the rack. She'll know that it's mine because right
below the seat, Dad engraved my name in the frame. I glance
hurriedly over my shoulder. No teachers in sight. Where are
they when you really need them?

I have to hurry to keep up to Mark's long strides. "Maybe
I'll just go back in the school until they're gone. They're from
the Comp. "

"I go to the Comp too. Are you scared of me?" He throws
a fleeting smile over his shoulder.

I ignore his question. "Look, one of those girls is very
pissed at me. She might have vandalized my bike."

Mark just keeps on walking. "All the more reason to talk
to them."

I finally cry out in exasperation. "She wants to beat me up!"

By now he is heading across the parking lot.

"You've got to be kidding!" I shout, stopping in my
tracks. "Please come back here!"

When Mark doesn't listen, I have no choice but to run and
catch up. I can see the group clearly now. Besides Marsha, Tyler
and Rick, there are two other girls I don't recognize. One of
them is skinny with long, greasy blonde hair. The other has a
tiny build and black dyed hair chopped off at varying lengths.

"Afternoon." Mark stops two metres from the group. "Can I see her bike?"

Marsha steps aside so we can see the front tire of my mountain bike, which is slashed. "Looks like somebody doesn't like you, little rich girl." She drops her cigarette butt and mashes it under her heel.

Mark moves closer and bends down to investigate the damage. He straightens up and stares down at Marsha. "Did you do this?"

I can't believe his nerve.

Marsha folds her arms across her chest. "It was flat when we got here."

I look at the neat slash in the tire, which was obviously made with a knife. "I must have run over some broken glass on the way to school this morning."

Mark raises a blond eyebrow but makes no comment.

"We were just waiting to give your little girlfriend a ride home," says Marsha. "From the looks of her, somebody's already given her an ass-kicking."

Girlfriend? I shoot Mark a quick glance.

"She's not going anywhere with you," Mark says quietly.

Rick looks Mark up and down. He's a lot scarier now than he was on Halloween night. "You want to make something of it, hockey boy?"

"I'll make out of it whatever you want," Mark says.

There is a long silence as Rick and Mark stare at one another. The tension in the air is tangible. I hold my breath.

"Let's get outta here," Marsha says suddenly. "It's too frickin' cold to stand around doing nothing." She starts walking toward Rick's car.

As the skinny blonde walks past me, she thrusts her face close to mine. "Don't think we're done with you. Just because you've got a boyfriend doesn't change anything. You're gonna pay for what you did to Marsha."

Wonderful. Marsha's got a sidekick too.

I watch the group climb into the car and peel out of the parking lot, spinning their wheels and spitting gravel. When they're gone, Mark says angrily, "They slashed your tire! Aren't you going to do anything about it?"

"No, and you aren't either. They've had their revenge. Now maybe they'll leave me alone."

Mark shakes his head. "They're not going to stop at vandalizing your bike. They won't be happy until they get you alone somewhere and beat the crap out of you. Haven't you told anybody about this?"

"I can handle it." Once the words are out of my mouth, I realize just how stupid they sound. If Mark and I hadn't struck up a conversation, Marsha and her pals would be beating the crap out of me right now. "I mean — Tara's dad knows about it."

"What did you do to piss them off, anyway?"

"I don't want to talk about it." I unlock my bike and roll it away from the stand.

"What're you doing?" he asks.

"What does it look like? I'm going to walk my bike home."

"Put it in the back of my truck. I'll give you a ride."

I argue with him half-heartedly for a minute, then watch him load my bike. I really don't want to run into Marsha's gang again on the way home. Besides, his half-ton is awesome. A shiny black Silverado with chrome hubcaps and running boards.

When we are both in the cab, he says, "Tell me what happened."

I shake my head. Tara probably knows everything. Let her tell him.

He smiles grimly. "All right, have it your way."

I speak only to give him directions to my house and to say one more thing. "Thanks for standing up for me today."

"You're welcome."

When we drive up to the house, Dad is standing in the open garage entrance, holding a hockey stick. What a great day for him to get home early from work. He's wearing an old Boston Bruins jersey and a pair of sweatpants that have definitely seen better days. It's too late to hope that Mark hasn't noticed him.

"Your dad looks kind of hostile," Mark comments as he lifts my bike out of the box. "Did I park too far from the side-walk?"

"Don't worry about it." I start to push the bike up the driveway. "Thanks for the ride."

"No problem. By the way, nice shiner."

My mouth is hanging open as I watch the Silverado drive away.

"Jessie!" Dad's voice interrupts my thoughts. "Who's the guy?"

"Tara Brewer's boyfriend."

He relaxes a little.

I park my bike in the garage, hoping he won't notice the damage. "Can I ask why you're dressed like that?" I gesture at his sweatpants, drawing his attention away from my bike.

Dad brightens immediately. "Good question. I bought you something at Canadian Tire." He opens the back of the Explorer and shows me the large cardboard box inside. It bears the picture of a street hockey net. "I thought you could use it to practise your shooting."

"Thanks, Dad." I help him lift the box out of the suv. "I might need some different equipment as well."

"Do you think you'll be able to stick it out for the entire season? You were pretty red in the face after your last game," he teases.

I don't take the bait. "I'd like to. It's really fun, Dad, and the girls are great."

As I help him assemble the net, I try to forget about Marsha and Rick – and Mark's amazing grey eyes. The guys with the great eyes are always taken.

chapter
nine

n Sunday night, an hour before game time, I lie on my bed and stare at my ceiling, trying to remember everything Steve and Mr. Kowalski told me about playing right wing.

I've got to catch some passes tonight. I'd sooner die than make a fool of myself in front of Kim. Also, if the girls thought I played well in my first game, I need to show them that I can improve, especially since I missed the Saturday practice.

I spent most of Saturday in Lignite, cleaning up the mess left by a disastrous Halloween. My job was painting picnic tables, which were purchased to replace the ones burned in the bonfire. There were a dozen other teenagers, including the boy I rode with in the cruiser. He didn't do anything except complain the whole time.

The experience was very humiliating, especially because the town employee in charge stared at me like I was a criminal. I wanted to tell him that I never did any-

thing, but what would be the point? Nobody believes anything I say anyway.

I gaze at the poster of Nickelback that hangs directly
above my bed. Maybe it's time to change the decor in here. I
make a mental note to find some pictures of Danielle Goyette
and Haley Wickenheiser. The Xtreme are always talking about
them.

I sit up, cross my legs and scrutinize my appearance in my
dresser mirror. Back in Saskatoon, Bailey used to tell me that
taupe eye shadow really brings out the green flecks in my
hazel eyes, but because most of the Xtreme don't wear makeup,
I won't put any on. I stare ruefully at my long brown hair,
which I have pulled into a high ponytail. Maybe I should cut
it short, like Tara's.

"Let's go, Jessie!" calls Dad from downstairs.

Showtime!

Later when I walk into the dressing room, I see that
watchful look in everyone's eyes again. What did I do
now?

As soon as I set down my bag and sticks, Shauna introduces me to Carla Bisson, a tall Aboriginal girl whose hands
are as big as my dad's.

"Nice to have another rookie on the team." Her low
voice booms in my ears.

At first I am confused. Then I remember that this is her first season playing girls' hockey. I nod shyly and start getting dressed.

"Hey, Carla!" Kathy gives her a friendly wave. "So you've finally decided to be a player instead of a fan." Then she adds in a more serious tone, "How did the Tigers do?"

"4 and 0." Carla has large white teeth and a beautiful smile. "Johnny played every game – even got to do some penalty killing. Daddy's little boy."

"Daddy's little boy is six feet tall – and gorgeous!" says Kathy.

"Keep your pants on, Parker," Shauna warns.

Teneil slides over to make room for Carla on the bench. "We did manage to whip Weyburn's butt without you."

Carla zips open her hockey bag and removes her shin pads. "So I heard."

"Where were you on Saturday?" Kathy looks at me while adjusting the fit of her jill. "If you want to play with us, you need to come to the practices – not just the games."

Tara speaks up immediately. "Jessie had a good reason for missing, but she can't tell you what it is. Cut her some slack, okay, Parker?"

Kathy tightens the strap on her hockey pants, still grumbling.

"We had way too many girls skipping practice last year." Shauna begins relacing one of her skates. "Luckily those girls decided not to play this season."

"Yeah, their parents were the ones who never wanted to go out of town," Miranda says. "They just couldn't understand why we didn't want to play boys' teams all the time."

"They'll drive their precious boys all over the flippin' countryside but complain about driving an hour for their daughters." Kathy shakes her head in disgust.

"Where's Randi?" Amber asks.

"She's in the other dressing room," Shauna says. "We're playing her Peewee boys' team tonight."

"Will she play with us again sometime?" Larissa asks.

Jennifer covers her dark hair with a bandana. "I sure hope so. I'd like to have four D all the time, instead of three."

"Having Carla on D will be great," says Shauna, nodding in the Aboriginal girl's direction. "Thanks for playing with us, Bisonhead."

Carla laughs. "I was getting sick of changing in the referee's room, the girls' washroom, the storage room, the broom closet..." Her voice trails off to a conspiratorial whisper. "Sometimes, if there were girls on the *other* team, my coach made me change with them."

"No way!" says Miranda. "That's going too far!!"

"Playing with the guys was awesome until last year," Carla says. "Those guys didn't respect the coach — or themselves. They dicked around during practice. And during games, they were more worried about picking fights than playing. I just got sick of it. I am definitely looking forward to this season," she adds slowly, "as long as we play lots."

I get the impression that Carla is dead serious about hockey.

"Mom's tried to schedule a game every week," Tara says hastily. "We've also entered some tournaments." She snaps her fingers. "Speaking of that, Dad says we need to decide soon if we want to enter the Regina tournament. And if we do enter, we need more players."

"Yeah, but who can we get?" Teneil asks. "We can't keep stealing girls from the Peewee boys' teams. It ticks off their coaches."

"Maybe we can find some more ice wreckers," Miranda teases.

"Ice wreckers?" I ask.

"Have you ever seen what the ice looks like after a figure skater is done making those figure eights?" Kathy climbs onto her imaginary soapbox. "Not to mention the flutzes — and flips — and camel toes."

The Xtreme explode into laughter.

"That's lutzes — and camel spins!" Teneil says when she is no longer doubled over. "Not camel toes! Who ever heard of a camel toe?"

Everyone is still howling when we leave the dressing room.

Once on the ice for the warm-up, I realize that if she isn't the Xtreme's best skater, Carla definitely has the hardest and most accurate shot. I also notice that Carla and Shauna are pretty thick. The two keep up a steady flow of conversation about the WHL teams, especially Medicine Hat and Moose Jaw.

While I'm waiting for my turn in a drill, I take a minute to look around and see if Kim's in the stands. I can't see her anywhere. Maybe she was just trying to psych me out so I wouldn't play well. Dad is standing in the bleachers with the other parents. He waves and gives me a thumbs-up.

I feel a little thrill of nervous excitement when my line is sent out to centre ice for the opening faceoff.

When the game gets underway, I soon discover that playing a Peewee boys' team is quite different from playing the Weyburn girls. The Ducks play every minute like it's over-time in the Stanley Cup final, and their mothers are even more competitive — if that is humanly possible.

"Hey, Number 10, pick on someone your own size!" A shrill voice shouts when Kathy goes into the corner with a little defenceman and, after a brief scuffle, knocks him down and emerges with the puck.

On the bench, I turn to Mr. Kowalski. "Should Kathy get a penalty for that?"

He shrugs his narrow shoulders. "I think the kid just

caught an edge, but with Kathy, you never know. She rather likes the crash and bang element of the game."

Mr. Kowalski doesn't seem to mind answering my questions, no matter how stupid they are. He explains the system that Steve uses for the forwards. First man in goes for the body, the second goes for the puck, and the third is the "high guy," ready to transition to defence if necessary. The more I watch Kathy, Amber, and Teneil's line, the more I see how the system works – and why it works so well. Particularly against the Ducks, a team which seems to be made up of "one-man shows."

Kathy scores two goals in the first period. The first is a beauty. Shauna gives her this perfect stretch pass that sends her on a breakaway. Kathy dekes the Ducks' goalie and roofs it on her backhand. Her second goal comes when Carla takes a slapshot from the blue line and Kathy tips it in from the slot. While the girls are congratulating one another, the Ducks' goaltender shouts something at Carla. It obviously rips her right off because she skates straight at him and cross-checks him into his own net. There are howls of protest from the Duck fans. Carla's face is dark as a thundercloud when she skates back to our players' box and slams her stick against the boards.

Through the grapevine, I hear that the goalie called her a "fat squaw." Carla, now sitting on the bench, is choking on tears of rage. Meanwhile the mothers of the Ducks are screaming for her blood.

"That's awful," I whisper to Larissa.

Larissa gives me a knowing look. "I've been called a stinky Paki and a terrorist. But it's all part of the game, right?"

Before I can say another word, Steve beckons to the referee, who is surrounded by the captains and assistant captains from both teams, all vying for his attention. The poor ref looks about seventeen and way over his head.

After listening to Steve, the ref skates over to the Ducks' bench and confers briefly with the coach, who looks shocked and apologetic.

"Well, that's something at least," says Tara when the Ducks' coach calls over his goaltender and chews on him for a while. The kid ends up with an unsportsmanlike penalty, which is served by one of his teammates. Carla gets two minutes for cross-checking and that seems to appease the Ducks' fans.

By the end of the first period, our team leads 3-2. Although I still haven't successfully caught a pass, I take some personal satisfaction in the fact that our line has not given up a goal. I feel surer of myself than I did in my first game, especially since there is no monster 44 tripping me at every faceoff. The Ducks swear at me and slash the backs of my legs, but it's kind of flattering that they regard me as a threat.

Early in the second period, Randi Hilderman, who plays centre with the Ducks, puts a move on Shauna and steps past the much-taller defenceman. In one neat motion, Randi shelfs the puck over Miranda's left shoulder.

"And that's why that girl should be playing with us all the time, right Dad?" Amber says as the scoreboard records the tie.

Mr. Kowalski nods, smiling.

By the halfway mark of the third period, the score is still tied at 3, but we are running out of gas. The Ducks look frustrated by the fact that even though they are outshooting us, they are unable to put the game away. Miranda, our ace in the hole, is having a brilliant game, stopping dozens of shots. With five minutes of stop time left to play, I am worn out.

Seconds later Amber hauls down a defenceman in the Ducks' end and receives a tripping penalty. Her line skates off the ice.

"Who stays off, Coach?" Tara asks Mr. Kowalski.

"I've had my share of ice time," Larissa pants. "Let Jessie go."

"Get out there, Larissa, and try to ice the puck, okay?"

Larissa reluctantly shuffles out of the box and skates over to the faceoff dot, where she lines up with Tara. "What's the big idea?" she shouts at Amber.

Amber smiles and waves cheerfully from behind the Plexiglas.

"I swear Amber tripped him on purpose," Mr. Kowalski says. "She knows better than to take a penalty in their end."

Fortunately, Tara wins the faceoff, moving the puck back to Jennifer, who passes across to Carla. Seeing that Larissa is open, Carla gives her a long pass. Because Tara is tied up, Larissa drives behind the net, a Duck dangling from each of her skinny arms.

"Now that's heads-up hockey!" Mr. Kowalski marvels as Larissa gives Tara, now free, a perfect pass in the high slot.

Tara one-times the shot and hits the Ducks' goaltender square in the chest. He goes down to try to cover the loose puck, but Larissa moves in front and jams it in.

Our bench goes nuts.

"We're up!" Mr. Kowalski shouts, hugging me and pounding me on the back.

"Man, I love short-handed goals!"

"Look at Larissa!" Kathy howls.

I look up in time to see Larissa's victory dance — the moonwalk.

Larissa, Tara, Carla and Jennifer skate past our bench before lining up again at centre ice. I wish I could've been on the ice for that goal.

My excitement is snuffed out when the Ducks' captain gets a breakaway and squeaks a shot through Miranda's legs — the good old five-hole. We are back to five on five, but the score is tied again.

"He's a cocky little mallard," observes Kathy as the Duck captain tosses his glove in the air and pretends to shoot it with the butt of his stick. "Somebody should pluck his feathers."

Steve walks down to our end of the bench. "And that somebody will not be you, Parker. We can't win this game from the penalty box." He pokes a big finger in her face, then crooks it at Amber, who is skating across the ice from the penalty box. "Have a seat, Amber." His dark blue eyes are piercing. "Kathy, Jessie, Teneil — you're up. Shauna and Jennifer, you're D. We'd like to beat this team, so don't do anything stupid out there."

I take my position at centre ice. I see that Kathy is now eye to eye with the Ducks' captain, who is grinning from ear to ear.

"Why don't you girls go play with your Barbies?" he snickers.

Kathy doesn't even blink. "You can shove Barbie up your ass," she says and knocks him flat the second the puck drops. The whistle blows again.

The referee points at Kathy and taps his chest, the signal for body contact. Kathy shrugs and skates to the penalty box.

Nervously, I look at our bench. Mr. Kowalski motions for me to stay on the ice. Steve has his back turned and appears to be muttering to himself.

"Looks like it's just you and me," Teneil says cheerfully. "Ready to kill your first penalty?"

I can't believe she isn't intimidated.

The Ducks' captain wins the faceoff, drawing the puck back to his left defenceman. I start backpedaling, hoping that the Ducks will decide to go to the other side of the ice. I groan when the defenceman passes up to the left winger, who bangs the puck off the boards and makes a deft move around me, leaving me high and dry.

"Backcheck!" Mr. Kowalski shouts.

Turning quickly, I head into my own end on the heels of the left winger, bearing down on him with each stride. I catch him just past the blue line and rub him out against the boards, managing to keep my feet while he goes down in a heap. When the puck pops into open ice, I go after it. Although I don't mean to, I run right over the Ducks' captain and accidentally knock the puck up to Teneil, who takes off up the ice on a breakaway.

Her rush is abruptly halted when one of the Ducks' defencemen hooks her from behind and hauls her down. Teneil manages to take out the Ducks' goalie and the net.

"Penalty shot!" my dad yells. "Open your eyes, ref!"

After the whistle, it takes several minutes for Teneil to untangle herself from the muddle of sticks and legs.

"No penalty shot, but someone is getting a penalty," Shauna observes as one of the referees skates over to the scorekeeper's box. "I hope it's not Teneil."

The call – hooking – goes against the Ducks. We are now even strength with two minutes left on the clock. The Ducks call a time out, and we all gather around Steve.

"Can I stay on, Coach?" Teneil asks.

Steve steps in before Mr. Kowalski has a chance to reply. "Teneil, set your fanny on the bench."

With a sheepish grin, Teneil sits down.

"Way to make contact, Jessie!" Miranda crows as Jennifer tosses her a water bottle.

"This game does not involve contact," Steve points out. "But I liked the way you took the defenceman off the puck. Nice move, Mac."

My ears perk up immediately. Has Steve just given me a nickname? I've never had one before – besides Jessie.

"What about the way she mowed down the ugly duckling at centre ice? Wasn't that great too?" Carla throws an arm around my shoulders.

"No." Steve seems to be on the verge of losing his temper. "That was charging. I'll thank you not to do that again when we're short-handed."

"It was an accident," I say meekly. "You can bench me if you want."

"No, you can stay out. Shauna, you take D with Carla. Tara, you're centre. As soon as Parker gets out of the penalty box, I'm moving Teneil to left wing."

"Don't you want Kathy out there for the power play?" asks Carla.

"Frankly — no. I've seen some poor decisions tonight — and Parker has made most of them. Remember to look after your man, and push them wide. Don't give them the middle of the ice."

The last two minutes of play slide by with agonizing slowness. Tara loses the faceoff to the Ducks' centreman, and we are soon scrambling in our own end, watching Miranda block shot after shot. For the first time I notice that some of the Ducks never seem to leave the ice. After the next line change, I ask Mr. Kowalski about it.

"They double-shift their better players, Jessie."

"But look at all the players they have." I point towards the Ducks' densely populated bench. "We have two lines — and they have more than enough for three."

"That's the way it is." Mr. Kowalski glances in Steve's direction. "You're lucky to have Steve for a coach."

"But you run the forwards most of the time. Thanks."

"You're welcome, but don't give me too much credit. When a team has a bench as short as ours, everybody plays."

When Kathy's penalty is over, Mr. Kowalski waves for her to come in, but Kathy pretends not to see him. Instead she jumps into the fray, roughly elbowing a Duck aside and digging the puck out from the boards. She throws it out to Carla, who sees that Tara is open and makes a beautiful pass, sending her into Duck territory on yet another breakaway. The Ducks, who have been playing deep in our end, are slow to react.

"Nice pass, Carla. Tara, don't look at the goalie this time," Mr. Kowalski murmurs.

Tara waits too long to make her move and runs out of room. She tries to deke but ends up stuffing the puck harmlessly into the goaltender's skates. The whistle blows. With only seventeen seconds remaining, Steve calls a time out.

"Parker, didn't you see us waving you off?" Steve thrusts a large gloved finger in Kathy's face. "What were you thinking?"

"I was thinking I was pretty fresh, and you'd need me out there for the power play," Kathy replies with annoying calmness. "Was I wrong?"

"Yes!" Steve thunders. "You're a loose cannon! At Tuesday practice, prepare to be bag skated! You're gonna beg me to let you take a break!"

I'm not sure what bag skating is, but it doesn't sound very nice. I'll have to ask Tara about it later.

The game concludes as a tie, but the Ducks are sullen and chippy when they line up to shake hands.

"They're acting like they lost!" I whisper to Tara as we step off the ice.

Before Tara can reply, Kathy jumps in. "Hey, gals, do you see who's here?"

I look hopefully in the direction Kathy is pointing but can't see Mark anywhere. Instead, I see Kim Scott and a slim, dark-haired girl talking to Miranda outside the dressing room.

"It's Kim and Jodi!" Tara says enthusiastically. "That's a good sign!"

"I'm gonna do some recruiting!" Kathy pushes past us and heads straight for the dark-haired girl, who I assume is Jodi Palmer.

So that's what the best female hockey player in the city looks like. Well, she's not very big. She's what Steve would call "light in the pants."

Kim catches me looking at them and pretends like she's gagging.

I quickly look away. Why doesn't she just grow up already?

Tara pulls me aside and speaks earnestly. "Don't let Jodi's size fool you." She pauses to pull off her helmet, revealing a sweat-soaked bandana. "She's a power forward, and she can play any position — except goal of course. Kim says she only made the AA team because her dad coaches. That's just jealousy talking. Kim's good too, but it was *her* dad coaching last year that got *her* on the team."

"Do you think Kim or Jodi would ever want to play with us?" I ask, dreading the answer.

Tara shakes her head. "It would take a miracle. Our team isn't competitive enough for either of them. Of course, I did hear a rumour that the Bantam A team only has twenty games scheduled this season – and one tournament. Kim won't like that much."

"Hi, rich girl. Long time no see."

I turn around. The skinny girl with the greasy blonde hair – the girl from the school parking lot – is standing behind me. Tyler is a few steps away, his forehead resting on the Plexiglas.

I swallow. My mouth suddenly feels very dry. "Hi."

Tyler keeps staring at the ice surface. He is obviously stoned.

"Been avoiding us?" Greasy Girl asks.

"It hasn't been that long," I reply.

"Jessie, the coaches want us in the dressing room," Tara insists. "Let's go."

Greasy Girl asks mockingly, "Is it Dykes Only?"

I pull up my cage so I can get a better look at her. "Is there something you want to say?"

"Actually, it's something Marsha wants to say." Her brown eyes, heavily coated with mascara and eyeliner, narrow. "You remember Marsha, don't you? She's pissed at you. Very pissed."

I lick my lips and dart a quick glance in Tyler's direction, but he seems hypnotized by the Zamboni circling the ice. "I never told the cops anything about Marsha."

"Right." Greasy Girl's voice is thick with sarcasm.

Steve sticks his head out of the dressing room. "Brewer! McIntyre! What's the holdup? Get your butts in here!"

"Let's go." Tara tugs on my arm.

I start backing away, letting Tara pull me along.

Greasy Girl swears at both of us, then stalks over to Tyler and curses him too for not being any help.

"Jessie, you need to talk to my dad about this," Tara whispers just before we enter the dressing room.

Both of my knees are shaking. I sit down on the bench and miss every word of Steve's post-game analysis. When the coaches leave, I strip off my equipment and avoid making eye contact with any of my teammates — especially Tara. I skip the showers and pull on my street clothes, even though my skin is damp and sticky. I am the first one out of the dressing room. Kim and Jodi are gone. No sign of Greasy Girl or Tyler.

Mom, Dad and Courtney are waiting for me in the rink lobby.

"Super game!" Mom pats me on the shoulder.

"Can we get something to eat?" Courtney crosses her arms over her chest. "I'm hungry!"

Dad reaches for my hockey bag. "I am so proud of you, kid!"

"Thanks. I'll carry my own bag." I brush past my family and head for the double exit doors. The night air feels cool on my hot cheeks.

Dad holds the door open for me so I can manoeuvre the bulky equipment bag through the narrow opening. "This girls' hockey is better than I expected. Your coach obviously knows a lot about the game."

"I'll tell him you said that." I suddenly feel very tired. "Let's go straight home."

chapter ten

I am breathless with excitement as I enter the Civic Auditorium the following Tuesday night with Kathy and Tara on my heels. It'll be the first time I get to see the AA Midget Bruins — and Mark Taylor — on the ice. Xtreme practice is finally over — thank goodness. Tonight I learned what bag skating is — wind sprints and more wind sprints. My legs feel like rubber. And trust Steve to take extra care in thinking up some fancy new drills on the very night I want to cut practice short. We also wasted precious minutes carrying our equipment out to our parents' vehicles and convincing my mother that she has time to come back and pick us up after the game.

We each pay a student admission, get our hands stamped, and grab a program.

"What's the rush, Jessie?" demands Tara, climbing the worn wooden steps that lead to the stands. "The first period won't even be over yet."

Kathy picks up the scent immediately. "I think Mac likes somebody! I wonder who?"

Crap! All I need is for Kathy to figure out I like Mark. Not that I intend to do anything about it. I like Tara too much.

As we enter the arena, I am relieved to see players on the ice. According to the clock, there are still five minutes left in the first period and no score.

Tara leads us to an empty section of the stands at the east end. She makes a beeline for the middle row and plops herself down, hanging her knees over the seat directly in front of her.

Trying not to look at Kathy, I settle myself next to Tara. "At least we haven't missed much of the game."

"Not much," agrees Tara. "It looks like the Midgets have got their work cut out for them."

"Look at the penalty box." Kathy nudges me with her elbow. Following the line of her gaze, I see that there are two Bruin players in the box. Worse yet, Mark's team is facing off in their own end. I watch in dismay as the Millionaires' centreman cross-checks the Bruins' centreman as soon as the puck is dropped.

"Are you blind, ref?" someone screams.

When there's no whistle, play continues in the Bruins' end, with defencemen and centreman scrambling to prevent a Melville goal. I kick myself for not asking Mark what number he wears. It's impossible to recognize him in his equipment, and I can hardly ask Kathy or Tara which one he is.

One of the penalties finally elapses, and a Bruin leaves the box. He heads into his own end to provide support, arriving just in time for Melville to score. A handful of fans cheer heartily. Must be from Melville.

"That's one for you, ref!" comes a strident voice from across the ice.

"That stinks," Kathy says.

"Good thing Mark's out of the box. He leads the team in penalty killing," says Tara.

Ah, yes. He's Number Four, and right now he is lining up at centre ice for the faceoff.

Kathy's eyes shine with sudden mischief. "Hey, Mac, who *do* you have the hots for? You sure were in a hurry to get here after practice."

I shrug one shoulder and focus on the ice, hoping Kathy doesn't notice my red cheeks.

Mark doesn't come off the ice for the entire penalty kill. His size gives him a distinct advantage. Plus, he has moves. He maintains control of the play – running down the clock, icing the puck, and rendering the Melville power play ineffective for two minutes. At equal strength, the Bruins are finally able to generate some offence, but as the horn sounds to conclude the first period, the score remains 1-0 for Melville.

"Mark sure can dangle, can't he?" Kathy ties the strings from her toque on top of her head. "What do you think, Mac? Think he's good enough to play for the Xtreme?"

Will she just quit that already? My cheeks are flaming. "I don't know much about defence." I watch the Bruins skate to the end of the ice to return to their dressing room. "Let's go get something to drink. I'm thirsty."

The three of us head down to the rink lobby. Once we get our drinks out of the machine, we go outside for a few minutes to grab some fresh air. Since smoking is not allowed in the building, a handful of adults are standing outside in the small parking lot that adjoins the arena, puffing on cigarettes and analyzing the first period.

The indigo sky is clear of clouds and full of stars. The temperature is several degrees below zero, and an icy breeze cuts through my fleece jacket. I tuck my hands inside my sleeves to keep them warm and listen with half an ear while Kathy and Tara discuss the possibility of Kim Scott and Jodi Palmer joining the team.

"Good thing Dad AP'ed them," Tara informs us.

"I'll say." Kathy takes a drink of her coke and burps. "Excuse me."

"What does AP mean?" I ask.

"They're Associated Players. That means they're registered with both our team and their Bantam boys' teams. They can play with us if they want to," Tara explains.

"I'd like Jodi to play, but I don't think Kim would be much fun." Kathy wears a very sour expression.

"Give her a chance," Tara replies. "She's not that bad — once you get past that chip on her shoulder. And she's a darned good athlete. She'd help the team."

"Well, I'm glad I don't see much of her anymore," I say, taking a sip of my drink.

"So Mark gave you a ride home from school on Thursday?" Tara asks suddenly.

I nearly choke on a mouthful of Powerade. "How did you know that?" I ask, after my coughing fit is over.

"He told me. He also told me about your bike — and those Comp kids. Jessie, you've got to talk to my dad."

Kathy is looking at me as if I have just confessed to a serial killing. "Will somebody fill me in, here?" She throws an arm around my shoulders. "Jessie, you have so many deep, dark secrets! And here I thought your life was b-o-r-i-n-g!"

Tara just stands there and looks at me expectantly.

Kathy lifts a strand of my hair and whispers in my ear. "Did he kiss you when he drove you home?"

"Shut up already!" I clap a hand over Kathy's mouth, then notice a number of people are staring at us with amused expressions. To my relief, most of them head back inside the arena for the beginning of the second period.

I move to follow them.

"Well, look who's here," says a sarcastic voice.

I reel as someone shoves me hard from behind. I would have fallen if Kathy hadn't caught me. Turning around, I am now face to face with Marsha and Greasy Girl and four others.

"How you been, rich girl?" Greasy Girl asks. "Told you Marsha was pissed."

Kathy thrusts me behind her.

"This doesn't involve you, Blondie," sneers Marsha. "If I were you, I'd go back inside."

"No way."

"There's more of us than there is of you," Greasy Girl points out. "You're all gonna get your asses kicked."

"I highly doubt that," Kathy replies in a tone I have never heard her use before. How can she not be as terrified as I am?

My heart pounds frantically. I search the ring of spectators for a friendly face but find none. They are all older girls — bored girls who get kicks from inflicting pain.

Tara exchanges a quick glance with Kathy before she begins backing away. "I sure don't want to get beaten up. I'm outta here."

I hear someone mutter something about Brewer's kid, and the girls part to let Tara through. One of them squawks like a chicken as Tara walks quickly towards the arena entrance. My heart sinks. She's just going to leave us here.

The girls immediately press closer to Kathy and me, their eyes glittering in anticipation.

"What about you, Blondie?" Greasy Girl thrusts her face at Kathy. "Are you gonna run too?"

"I have this thing called personal space," Kathy says coolly, "and you are in it right now."

"So?" Greasy Girl counters.

"So, I'm ready any time you are — or do you have to go home and wash your hair first?"

Greasy Girl takes a swing, but Kathy easily sidesteps the blow. She brings her elbow down on the back of Greasy Girl's head and knocks her off balance. Then Kathy grabs the hem of Greasy Girl's sweatshirt with both hands and pulls it over her head, trapping her arms and blindfolding her. Greasy Girl screams obscenities and tries to kick Kathy in the shins, but Kathy easily evades her flailing feet and wrestles her to the ground. She twists Greasy Girl's arm behind her back and scissors her legs to stop them from kicking. The rest of the girls — including Marsha — start laughing.

Greasy Girl is spewing a deluge of swear words that would make a referee blush.

"Give it up, Bonnie!" Marsha shouts. "You're done!" Then she turns and stares at me. Only a few feet separate us.

"You ready to take what you've got coming?" she asks.

And something in me just snaps.

I start singing "The Junior Birdsmen," a song Keisha and I learned at Pike Lake Bible Camp three summers ago. "Up in the air, the Junior Birdsmen! Up in the air, and upside down! Up in the air, the Junior Birdsmen, with their noses to the ground!"

I throw in all the actions too, including the parts where I pretend I'm an airplane soaring close to earth and a pilot wearing goggles. The performance definitely sets Marsha back. She glances over her shoulder at the others and when our eyes meet again, she looks confused.

Even though I'm totally out of breath, I just keep on singing. The cold air is making my voice all phlegmy, but I don't care. I guess it's my fear and helplessness and anger gushing out all at once.

Halfway through the song, I look over at Kathy to see how she's taking this. She's still lying on top of Greasy Girl, but Greasy Girl has managed to wriggle her head free of her sweatshirt. Both of them are staring like a pair of bigmouth bass. Marsha's friends are laughing, pointing at me, and talking amongst themselves.

I finally run out of verses and stop, my breathing deep and ragged. My heart is pounding like crazy.

Marsha just stares at me. "Are you frickin' nuts?" she asks after a long moment.

"I guess I am." I'm gasping for air, and my nose is running. "But I never called you a 'fat pig,' Marsha. I never even saw you before Halloween night! And I'm not crazy enough to tell the cops about you. Honest." The effort of talking makes me light-headed.

"You expect us to believe that?" Marsha demands.

"You've got a bad reputation, Marsha. And a girl at school who hates me knows it. She started this whole thing by spreading rumours on MSN. And I'm guessing she also let you know I'd be home alone on Halloween night."

"I don't give a rat's ass about any of this," Marsha says. "You —"

Out of the blue the arena doors fly open and Tara dashes out, with three men in her wake. They skid to a halt as soon as they spot us. I've never been so glad to see three total strangers in my life. I should have guessed that Tara wouldn't throw me to the wolves.

"Hey!" one of the men shouts. "What's going on here?"

Kathy abruptly stands up and releases Greasy Girl, who backs toward Marsha and the others, waving her middle finger like a weapon.

The men step towards us.

Marsha drops a few F-bombs, then gestures to her posse. With Tara and the rest of the cavalry here, the girls cross the access road.

"Don't you walk away on me!" I scream. "If you walk away on me now, you can't ever beat me up!"

"Don't count on it!" Marsha yells back.

The six of them climb into a beat-up half-ton with no shocks and drive away.

"Is this one of them?" A heavy-set man points at Kathy.

"No, that's Kathy Parker!" Tara says.

Kathy smiles and waves a hand in acknowledgment, then looks down in disgust at her mud-stained clothes. "Aw, my new hoodie."

Tara stares at me in amazement. "Jessie, are you all right?"

"I'm fine."

One of the men asks, "Were those girls threatening you?"

"Yes, but you got here before they could do anything. Thanks."

"If I were you, I'd be reporting this to the authorities," another one says. "Do you need a ride home?"

"I'm okay, really." I'm lying, of course. My knees are shaking so hard I can barely stand.

The men hang around for a while, asking for more details and offering advice. Then from inside the arena, we hear an air horn and loud cheering and "Zombie Nation" on the loudspeakers — sure signs of a Bruin goal. In a minute, the men are gone.

Kathy drapes an arm around my neck. "Nice voice, Mac, but don't give up your day job."

Tara looks at us both helplessly. "What happened out here?"

Kathy starts laughing, so I have to explain. "Mrs. Wright told me that when someone's harassing you, you should distract them, so I just started singing."

Tara's eyebrows shoot skyward. "What on earth did you sing?"

"Some corny song I learned at camp. It was the first thing I could think of."

"It was *really* bad, but sooo awesome!" Kathy hugs me close. "If I'd had a camera, that performance would be on YouTube tonight!"

My teeth are chattering by now. Good thing for Kathy's grip on my shoulders or I'd collapse. "Thanks a lot — both of you. If you hadn't been around, I would have been dead meat."

"Are you kidding?" Kathy asks. "Every kid at school should see the way you stood up to those girls! I'd give a million bucks to have a picture of Schwartz's face when you started singing!"

I am really relieved when Tara steps in. "I think you should quit talking about it, Kathy. " She looks me right in the eye. "Jessie, do you want to call your parents?"

"Let's just go watch the rest of the game. I'd really like to sit down."

As we walk back inside the Civic, I am still thinking about Marsha's last words. Maybe it is time to talk to Steve.

chapter
eleven

hen I'm on MSN on Thursday after supper, Tara asks if I want to go to the show Friday night. I've been talking to most of the Xtreme on MSN ever since I joined the team, but this is the first time Tara's asked me to do something that's not related to hockey.

Then she tells me that Brian, Shauna, Miranda, Teneil, Nathan and Mark are coming along.

All of a sudden my heart starts racing, and I get butterflies.

I tell her I can go — even though I know I'm going to have to do a major con job on Mom and Dad. I'll out-and-out lie if I have to.

That's when Tara asks me if it's true that my dad is territorial — not that she spells territorial right. Tara works really hard at school, but spelling is not one of her strong points.

I guess she and Mark must talk about everything — even me.

I have my work cut out convincing my parents to let me go to the show. Neither of them is sure how long I'm supposed to be grounded — or from what. Finally, they agree to let me go, as long as Dad can drop me off at the theatre and meet the boys first.

"I'm giving you my cellphone so you can call when you're ready to come home," he says on our way downtown. "You're also to use it if you have an emergency."

Hmm. An emergency would be running into Marsha in the back alley behind the theatre.

I stare balefully at the ugly black monstrosity sitting on the dash. It's circa twentieth century. General Patton probably used the same model during the conquest of Italy. With any luck no one will see me using it.

"How long did you say the movie is?"

I roll my eyes and stare out the side window of the Explorer, feeling like a prisoner. If he and Mom knew what happened last Tuesday at the Civic, they would have kittens.

"So you're sure none of these boys are interested in you?" Dad asks for the hundredth time.

"I told you already — Mark is going out with Tara. And Brian is Shauna's boyfriend. I don't know anything about Nathan except he plays hockey with the other two." I fail to keep the irritation out of my voice.

"Don't you give me attitude, young lady," he says in a warning tone. "You're lucky to be going out at all."

"I know that." I slump down in the seat and fold my arms across my chest. "Dad, this is the first time I've gone out with friends since I got here. Can't I enjoy myself?"

He reaches over and squeezes my hand. "Of course you can. Just don't expect me to come pick you up at the police station at the end of your evening."

The interrogation in front of the movie theatre isn't as bad as I expected. Dad at least pretends to be cool about the whole thing.

It turns out Tara isn't able to come to the show.

"She texted me on the way here. Her mom got called to work at the hospital, and Tara has to babysit the rug rats," explains Teneil. "She's very PO'd."

When we go inside, I pay my own way, but Mark insists on buying my popcorn and drink, which is strange because he doesn't offer to pay for anyone else's. Then he sits right next to me while Miranda and Teneil sit behind us, and Nathan, Brian, and Shauna sit next to him. Before the movie starts, he asks me all these questions about Saskatoon and ringette and everything else you can imagine. I keep looking back at the girls to see if they're ticked, but they keep chatting it up. Once Teneil catches me looking at her, and she gives me this big wink. What's with her, I wonder.

A few minutes before the show is scheduled to begin, Mark decides to go for more popcorn – seeing as how Brian and Nathan have finished theirs and devoured half of his. While he's gone, Kim and her flunkie Natalie Wilgenbush come up the aisle. Kim spots me right away. Great.

"Decided to get out of the house, did you?" Kim gestures at the empty seat beside me. "Too bad you don't have any friends. Was Marsha busy tonight?"

"How the heck would I know? She's your buddy – not mine," I reply.

"I saw your game against the Peewee boys on Sunday." Kim exchanges a nasty look with Natalie. "I have just one word to describe it. Pathetic."

Teneil leans over the back of my seat and offers me a piece of licorice. "Oh, hi, Kim," she says. "Couldn't get a date tonight?"

Kim shoots her a dirty look. "I've got a hockey tournament tomorrow in Weyburn. I don't need any distractions."

"Wow, a hockey tournament." Teneil takes a bite of her licorice and chews it thoughtfully before saying, "Sure hope you get some ice time. Heard you only got three shifts in your last game."

How does everybody know this stuff? I wonder. I sure wish I knew it.

Mark returns from the concession and stepping past Kim, slips into his seat. "Want some?" he asks, holding up a large bucket of popcorn.

Naturally, Nathan and Brian lean over and dig in.

Awesome. Hollywood couldn't write a better script. I would give a million bucks to have a picture of Kim's and Natalie's faces. They just stare at Mark, their mouths opening and closing like goldfish.

"Hi, Mark," Kim says after a while.

"How are you doing, Kim?" Mark asks, slapping Brian's hand away.

Kim smiles brightly. "Great! Well, we gotta take a leak before the show starts! See ya!"

Very classy, Kim. You always were a smooth talker.

She and Natalie take off up the aisle. Then I start thinking about what they'll say to Tara at school on Monday. I never should have let him sit next to me.

The theatre darkens, and the previews begin.

The movie turns out to be boring. It's an action adventure with far too much stuff blowing up, but the guys seem to like it. I can't concentrate on a single word of dialogue — not with Mark sitting beside me. I keep thinking about what Tara would say if she could see us right now.

Afterward, while we're standing on the street corner, everyone decides to go to a party at Kathy's. Even though I'd like to go too, I dutifully phone Dad and tell him to come pick me up. They all stare at Dad's cellphone like it came from another planet, but no one says anything — thank goodness.

"I'm really tired," I say to Miranda. "You guys go ahead and have a good time. My dad will be here any minute."

Mark says, "I'll keep you company until your dad gets here. Brian can fit everyone in his car."

Miranda gives me a hug. "See you tomorrow at practice, girl. Remember Sunday's game is in Lignite. And – believe it or not – Mrs. Brewer got us two hours of ice time."

When everyone is gone, I stand there, shivering in my fleece, feeling like a fool.

"Do you want to wait in my truck?" Mark asks. "It's warmer."

As much as I'd like to do just that, my dad will ground me for life if he catches me in Mark's half-ton again. Not to mention what Tara would think.

"I'm fine. Thanks." I fold my arms around my chest and shove my bare hands in my armpits to keep them warm.

"Do I make you feel uncomfortable or something?" Mark asks out of the blue.

"What?"

"All night you've hardly listened to a word I've said. Did I do something wrong?"

I look at him in surprise. "Of course not." Out with it, I think to myself. Just do it. I take a deep breath. "I don't get it, that's all. Why are you paying so much attention to me?"

He puffs his cheeks and lets out his breath in a large, vapoury cloud. "Well, that's blunt." He removes his hat and rubs his scalp. "I like you – that's all. I enjoyed talking to you at the school the other day, and I'd like to get to know you better. I think you're interesting and – pretty."

A wave of anger washes away my nervousness. "How can you say that?"

"Huh?"

I turn and face him, placing my hands on my hips. "Just what are you trying to do?"

His eyes get very wide, and he shakes his head. "I'm trying to ask you out. I didn't know you'd get so touchy."

"Touchy?" I am amazed at his nerve. "Just who do you think you are, anyway?"

At that very moment the Explorer pulls up to the curb, and the passenger side window descends. "Ready to go, Jessie?" my dad asks, leaning across the seat. He doesn't look happy.

"Sure." I open the door and climb in.

"See you, Jessie," Mark says.

He really looks hurt. I can't imagine why. What a scumbag. I give him a curt nod, and we drive away.

"Where are the other girls?" Dad's gripping the steering wheel with both hands – a bad sign.

"They went to a party."

"I see." His right thumb starts tapping the wheel. "How old is this Mark anyway?"

"I don't know, and I don't care. He's a jerk. Can we just go home?"

Before practice the next day, I corner Steve in the lobby and tell him about the incident outside the Civic on Tuesday night.

"Mac, I feel partially responsible for this." His voice sounds rough. "Tara and Mark have both told me about the way Schultz has been harassing you. And you ignoring it will not make it go away. Do you want to press charges?"

"For what?" I ask him. "She's only made threats. I can't prove she wrecked my bike."

"Those threats are definitely grounds for pressing charges. And you need to know those bullies are not going to leave you alone until you stand up to them."

I have a sneaking suspicion that I have already done that.

Steve's next statement nearly blows me away. "Maybe you better let me handle it."

I really hope he's not going to tell my parents. I'll never get out of the house again if they find out. "What are you going to do?" I ask.

"You'll see. In the meantime, hang around after practice for a few minutes. I'm going to give you some pointers on self-defence."

Later, while I'm unpacking my equipment, Tara decides to conduct her own interrogation. "So — what's going on with you and Mark?" She looks really ticked.

It's what I've been dreading, but I can't believe she is airing our dirty laundry in front of the entire team. I finally make some friends in this godforsaken city, and one cute guy with an earring's got to screw it up. "Nothing," I say emphatically.

She has no trouble hearing me because there's dead silence. All the girls are staring at us.

Tara gives me a sideways glance. "Nothing? Is that all you have to say?"

I shrug and wonder how much I should tell her about her slimy boyfriend.

Then she drops the bombshell. "Jessie, do you know how many girls would kill to go out with Mark?"

"What?"

Kathy waves an arm in the air. "I'm a huge fan. Huge."

"He is most definitely hot," says Jennifer.

"What are you talking about?" I stand up right in front of Tara. I'm wearing only my sports bra and boxers, but I don't care. "He asked me out! I didn't ask him!"

"And that's as it should be," says Teneil. "At least according to my grandma."

I begin to get the uncomfortable feeling that there's

something important I'm missing. I take a deep breath. "Tara, did you break up with Mark?"

Her eyes get wide, and then she bursts into laughter. Not only her — the entire dressing room.

"What's so funny?" I slowly turn around and look at everyone. "What's going on?"

Kathy wipes the smile off her face and assumes an expression of mock seriousness. She places her hands on my shoulders and says very slowly and deliberately, as if I'm deaf, "Jessie, Mark is Tara's *cousin.*"

I groan and close my eyes, trying to remember what I said to Mark after the movie. Did I actually call him a scumbag, or did I just think it?

"It's okay, everybody," says Shauna, smiling. "Apparently in Saskatoon people date their cousins."

"Will you tell him, Tara?" I plead. "Promise me you'll tell him I didn't know!"

Chuckling, Tara shakes her head and slumps down on the bench. "No, Jessie, you're going to tell him yourself. Good luck!"

It's a miracle, but somehow I manage to survive the entire hockey practice without killing myself.

chapter twelve

can't suck up the courage to call Mark. I've never phoned a guy in Grade Eleven – much less a guy who's got his own vehicle.

Maybe he'll be at our game, I tell myself on the way to Lignite on Sunday. I'll talk to him as soon as it's over.

While I'm putting on my equipment, I ask Tara if Mark's coming.

She gives me a sympathetic look. "I doubt it. He's got practice tonight."

I'll call him tomorrow, I promise myself.

Then I notice how quiet it is in the dressing room, and I promptly forget about Mark. It's obvious even to me that tonight's game against the Southern Wildcats is an important one.

After we're dressed, Steve tells me I'm playing right wing on Kathy and Teneil's line. When I ask him why, he says, "You've had a chance to learn the game. I want to see what'll happen if I move you around. Take it as a compliment."

I try to. I just wish I could get rid of this feeling I'm going to let the Xtreme down.

"Dad thinks the Wildcats are the best girls' team in the southeast," Tara says when we step onto the ice for the pre-game warm-up. "We never beat them last year, but he thinks we will tonight."

I try to concentrate on the drills, but my eyes keep travelling to the other end of the ice. Even to my inexperienced eye, I can see there's a huge difference between the Wildcats and us.

"They're all good skaters," I say to Carla, "and they've all got slapshots! How are we going to beat them?"

Carla gives me a long look. "I guess we can try to score on them. That might help."

By the time our warm-up is over, I notice a large number of fans crowded around the boards – people of all ages.

"Why are there so many people here?" I ask Jennifer.

"They're nuts about hockey in this town," she replies. "Ain't it great?"

Next I notice that we have three officials on the ice. I ask Mr. Kowalski about this.

"The Wildcats are very physical," he explains. "Steve thought a two-man system would be inadequate. Keep your head up."

Mr. Kowalski must be some kind of oracle, because after five minutes, my forearms are so badly bruised and achy it hurts to hold my stick. Kathy's been hooked and held so much she can't make any headway on the ice. Jennifer and a Wildcat winger take a roughing penalty for having a shoving match in Miranda's goal crease.

By the midway point of the first period, the language on the bench and on the ice is foul. I cannot believe the words coming out of sweet little Amber Kowalski's mouth.

The fans love it when Kathy catches one of the Wildcat forwards with her head down at centre ice and throws a text-book shoulder into her. By the end of the first period, the Xtreme have earned four penalties, and the Wildcats five. The score is tied at zero.

"Don't let them intimidate you, but don't stoop to their level," Steve tells us in the dressing room. "Use your heads."

Both teams are better behaved in the second period, and the pace of the game accelerates. For the first time this year, I get to experience end-to-end action and learn how to transition quickly.

Still, Teneil manages to find time between shifts to razz me a little. "Drove past your place the other day with my older sister. Your dad was out shovelling the walk."

"So?"

"He was wearing these awesome sweatpants. Man, did he look hot."

I know which sweatpants she is referring to and what's coming next. The girls are on this kick lately of bugging me about my dad.

"My sister wants to know if she can ask him out. Think your mom would mind?"

"Shut up!"

Early in the period, one of Kathy's passes lands right on my blade, and I'm thrilled when I manage to carry the puck a few feet before passing cross-ice to Teneil. Near the hash marks, Teneil takes a hard wrist shot, but the goalie easily deflects it. The Wildcat centreman picks up the puck, and in a split second, I am backchecking in the neutral zone.

"I'm going to start calling you the Mailman," Kathy tells me later as she smacks me on the helmet. "Nice delivery!"

Because the Wildcat defence plays body position so well, we are usually restricted to one shot on net. Fortunately, the reverse is also true. Miranda is having a stellar game, as are Carla, Shauna and Jennifer.

With half a minute left in the second period, my line has a faceoff just outside our own blue line. Kathy loses the draw, but Carla outmuscles the Wildcat centreman for control of the puck. She banks it off the boards toward me, and I get a lucky bounce. I manage to make a move around the Wildcat left winger, but I can feel the centreman breathing right down my neck. There's nothing but one defenceman between me and the Wildcat goaltender. I accelerate quickly, pushing the puck ahead of me. Out of the corner of my eye, I can see Kathy and Teneil are both open. I give Kathy a pass, narrowly avoiding an offside call, then drive to the net. The defenceman tries to poke-check Kathy while the goalie shifts her body in Kathy's direction. When Kathy slides the puck back to me — a perfect pass — I shoot it into a wide open net. Child's play.

The red light goes on, and the Lignite fans erupt.

I have just scored my first goal.

Kathy and Teneil are pounding me on the back and hooting in my ear.

"Way to be, Mailman!" Kathy screams.

My heart is bursting as I lead the skate past our bench to the rollicking beat of Gary Glitter.

However, in the third period the Wildcats score two unanswered goals, and we go down to defeat 2-1.

There are a few sour grapes in the dressing room afterward. Kathy in particular has a tough time handling the loss.

"I hate losing to them!" she rages.

Steve is his usual philosophical self. "The highs can't be too high, and the lows can't be too low. It's early in the season, and we'll beat them when it really counts. You all played awesome for fifty-five minutes. We just had a few breakdowns in the third period." He pulls out his clipboard and pencil.

"Now – on to more important business. Who knows for sure that they're coming to Regina in three weeks?"

I eagerly nod my head when he calls my name. Mom and I are going to drive to Regina with Teneil and Mrs. Howard in their Suburban and share a hotel room. Dad will stay home and look after Courtney, who has a skating competition that weekend. I get the feeling he'd much rather watch me play in Regina.

Not long after the coaches leave the dressing room, we hear water running in the shower room and Wildcats crowing about their victory.

"I can't believe they expect us to shower together," Kathy says. "Couldn't they have given the Wildcats a different dressing room?"

"Watch this!" Jennifer jumps up and runs over to the sink in the corner. Grinning, she turns on the hot water full blast, then throws back her head and cackles like the Wicked Witch of the West.

"What are you doing?" someone asks.

"Just wait!"

In a minute, the laughter next door changes to loud screams.

"Nothing like a little ice-cold water to help speed up the cooling-down phase of aerobic activity," Jennifer says.

On the drive back to Estevan, Mom asks, "Which weekend were you planning to go to Saskatoon?"

When I tell her, she turns right around in her seat and looks at me. "Isn't that the same weekend as the Regina tournament?"

Crap! Why does everything have to fall on the same weekend? I'd made plans to stay at Bailey's house and go to a dance at Walter Murray. It was going to be the perfect opportunity to visit all my old friends.

I can see Dad's face in the rear-view mirror when he asks, "Well, what's it gonna be, kid? Regina or Saskatoon?"

It seems like the only time I even think about Bailey, Keisha and Tayja is when I'm talking to them on MSN. I'm always telling them how much I miss them and how I wish I was back in Saskatoon. But the truth is — I spend more time thinking about hockey and hanging out with Tara and Shauna at school. It makes me feel guilty — like I'm somehow betraying the Fab Four — but I know there's no way I'm missing that tournament in Regina.

"I don't want to let my team down," I say at last. "Can we go to Saskatoon some other time?"

"Of course," Mom says, "if we can find a weekend when we're not tied up with hockey or figure skating. But you better let Bailey know as soon as you get home." She looks really pleased with my decision. I think she's looking forward to the tournament as much as I am.

I can't resist saying, "You know, if I had a cellphone of my own, I could just text Bailey right now."

As usual, Mom pretends not to hear. I'll probably be wearing Depends before I get my own phone.

Before the end of November, we play Weyburn, Qu'Appelle and Melita, winning all three games, then lose 6-0 to the Notre Dame B team. They're all away games, and Mark doesn't come to any of them. Tara tells me his team has a busy schedule with tournaments and league games every weekend and at least two practices a week. She keeps telling me to call him, but the more time that passes, the harder it is.

I'm a coward. And I can't do a thing about it.

After one of our practices, Steve gives me some pointers on self-defence. Most of them involve breaking out of holds and creating opportunities to run, seeing as how I'd be an idiot to take on Marsha and her friends at once. He also makes me promise never to go anywhere alone — even in broad daylight.

I've convinced Mom and Dad that it's better for me and my sister to eat lunch at school. Now I don't have to make that scary walk between home and Courtney's elementary school, right across the street from EJH, every noon hour. I'd rather face the occasional taunt from Kim or Natalie on the playground than run into Marsha when I've got my little sister tagging along. And since I've started hanging out with Tara and Shauna, I don't get harassed at school anymore. Mrs. Wright was really smart to put me in their homeroom.

Mom picks Courtney and me up at three thirty most days to drive Courtney to figure skating, so I don't have to worry about seeing Marsha after school. And I do most of my homework while Courtney's on the ice, so my marks aren't too bad on my first report card.

Steve's not the only one interested in my self-preservation. Kathy pulls me aside and shows me a few things as well.

"Of course, I've never actually *fought* anyone on the ice," Kathy says modestly. "My big brother and I just watch the highlights on TSN and then wrestle in the living room."

One time Marsha shows up during a practice and watches me from the other side of the glass. It freaks me out, but there's no sign of her afterward. I see her in the mall a few times too, but luckily I'm with Mom or Dad, so she keeps her distance. The way that she stares at me is really creepy though.

The kids at school eventually start talking to me, even when I'm not with Shauna or Tara, and I get the feeling that I'm on the road back to popularity. Well, not popularity exactly. I don't want to be popular. I'd like to be somewhere halfway between popular and totally unpopular. High-profile girls like Kim and Natalie don't seem happy because they're always mad at somebody. Anyway I'm too busy with school and hockey to worry about who's going out with who and stuff like that.

And wonder of all wonders, my parents start to loosen up. On Teneil's fourteenth birthday, she's having a party and a sleepover, and I get to go.

At our final practice before the Regina tournament, our dressing room is buzzing with details — what teams will be there, how the Xtreme did against them last year, who's sharing a hotel room. It all sounds like one great road trip.

"Do you usually win this tournament?" I ask when there's a lull in the conversation.

Everyone looks at me like I've got an arm growing from the top of my head.

"We've never even won a *game* in Regina," Miranda says at last. "We usually get slaughtered."

News to me, I can tell you. "So what's all the hype about?" I ask.

"Every year, we get a little better," Kathy says. "And now we've finally got a decent defence to go along with our awesome offence."

"Are you saying our defence sucked last year?" Shauna asks.

I can tell she's a mighty unhappy camper.

"Is that what I said?" Kathy tilts her head at an absurd

angle. "I meant to say we've always had an outstanding defence, but our offence often fails to score at..."

"Crucial turning points," Teneil finishes for her.

"Exactly," Kathy says.

"Well, this year, there's me and Carla and Jessie on the roster, and I think we're gonna win that tournament," says Jennifer. "Those Regina teams will never know what hit them."

"This year maybe we'll win one game," corrects Shauna.

"Now, that would be sweet," says Miranda.

At home, I spend every spare minute playing street hockey with my dad or with the eleven-year-old twin boys who live next door. The twins are endlessly amused by my efforts to take slapshots and raise the puck.

"You're not bad – for a girl," one of them observes after I miss the top corner of the net for the hundredth time. "A little more practice – and you'll be average."

"Thanks," I reply. "Average will be good enough for now."

chapter *thirteen*

I 've got a little surprise for you, girls." Mrs. Brewer smiles broadly as she enters our dressing room in Regina's Balfour Arena. "Steve knew you didn't want to come to this tournament short-handed, so he picked up an extra player."

"We already know about Randi," says Amber. "She's coming for our game tomorrow morning, right?"

"I'm not talking about Randi."

The door opens, and right on cue, Kim Scott walks in, carrying sticks in one hand and an equipment bag in the other.

You could hear a pin drop in our dressing room. I'm not kidding.

"Hey, Kim!" Shauna gives a friendly wave.

Kim leans her sticks against the wall beside a dozen others, and then deposits her bag in the centre of the room.

"Nice to have ya here." Miranda slides over to make room on the bench.

Kim shrugs and sits down next to Miranda. "I'm just here because Steve said you needed another D, and I'm not busy this weekend."

"That's a good enough reason," says Shauna. "We sure need you, Kim. Don't we, girls?"

Everyone nods and murmurs agreement – except for me.

Mrs. Brewer looks around the room and counts heads. "Isn't Larissa here yet?" she asks when she's done. "That girl is always late! Well, hurry up and get dressed, ladies. Steve wants to get in here and talk strategy."

From her flushed face, I can tell she is as nervous and excited as we are.

Then it dawns on me that, in spite of all their reserve and self-control, Steve and Mr. Kowalski want to beat a Regina team just as badly as we do. I make a decision right then and there to do my best to steer clear of Kim and not create any unnecessary tension in the dressing room or on the bench. It's the least I can do.

"How's Jodi doing?" Miranda asks after Mrs. Brewer is gone. "I hear she has to wear one of those straitjacket things – even when she goes to bed. Man, that would suck."

"Why does she have to wear one of those?" Amber asks.

Kim looks at Amber as if she's the dumbest person on the face of the earth. "Haven't you heard? She broke her collarbone when she got checked from behind in that game against Yorkton."

"Do you mean Jodi Palmer?" I ask, surprised.

"Of course I mean Jodi Palmer!" Kim says harshly. "Do you know another Jodi who plays hockey?"

"I guess she's still pretty sore, huh?" Jennifer asks, rummaging around in her hockey bag.

Carla whistles. "I'm glad I'm not in her shoes."

"You said it," says Kathy.

"Do you know everyone here, Kim?" Shauna inquires.

Kim looks around the room slowly, examining every face. When it's my turn, her eyes slide right over me, as if I'm not even there. "I think so," she says at last. "Everybody knows me, right?"

The girls bob their heads, then resume dressing.

That's when Larissa comes barrelling in. She trips over a skate and ends up sprawled in a heap on top of her equipment bag.

"Sorry I'm late, guys!" she gasps. "Dad had to deliver a baby, and —"

"Crap!" Jennifer explodes.

"What's wrong?" Tara asks.

"I forgot my jill! It isn't in my bag anywhere!" Jennifer gives her bag an angry kick with her bare foot and throws her can across the dressing room. It narrowly misses hitting Larissa.

"Hey, watch it!" Larissa shouts.

"Sorry."

"Are you sure you don't have it?" Carla asks.

"Of course I'm sure."

"Well, put your top stuff on," says Shauna. "When Tara's mom comes back, we'll tell her to borrow a jill from one of the other teams."

"But I can't!" Jennifer wails. "I always put on my jill first — then my left sock, shin pad, and skate. Then I do my right side."

"Got a pair of boxers?" Carla stands up and moves toward Jennifer, carrying a roll of sock tape and Jennifer's can.

Jennifer looks at Carla suspiciously. "Yes."

"Put 'em on."

"What are you gonna do?" Jennifer looks nervous, but she follows Carla's instructions.

"My brother had to do this once. Here, hold your can right there." While Jennifer holds the can in place on her pelvis, Carla begins taping it to her boxer shorts amidst our laughter and obscene suggestions. Afterward, Kathy cranks up the ghetto blaster, and Jennifer does a sideways shuffle dance around the room to make sure the can won't come loose. Meanwhile Larissa is tearing off her street clothes and yanking on her equipment in record time.

Out of the blue Kim shouts, "Hey, gals, did you know the AA Midgets are playing at the Agridome?"

That girl just has to be the center of attention, I think to myself. Tara told me a week ago that Mark's team would be in Regina this weekend, but it doesn't matter. I haven't even seen him since we went to that movie. We may be in the same city, but we're playing in two different tournaments and staying in two different hotels. He might as well be playing hockey on the moon.

"Mark told me Swift Current's their biggest competition in the round robin," Kim says. "I hope I get to see at least one of his games. He said he'd try to come to one of mine."

Horrified, I shoot a questioning glance at Tara, but she looks away and starts lacing one of her skates. My heart starts pounding. Does this mean what I think it means?

Kim goes on and on about Mark for the next ten minutes. I bet she uses his name a hundred times. Everyone listens politely for a bit. Then Shauna and Tara each make valiant efforts to change the subject. Both times, Kim goes right back to Mark, just like a golden retriever pointing at a dead duck. It's sickening.

I bite the inside of my cheek and count to ten. After a while I find it more satisfying to imagine myself taking slapshots at Kim's head.

"Mark says he likes the fact there's no contact in girls' hockey." Kim pulls on her helmet. "He says it makes the game faster paced. Now, that's the one thing we don't agree on."

Shut up, already! Put in your mouthguard!

Kathy tugs off her gloves and throws a few playful punches. "There's always contact, Kim. Some of us have a habit of running into the opposition now and then."

"I run into the opposition lots." Kim smiles smugly. "Mark says I can throw hits as good as anybody on his team."

She's lying, and I know it. Tara says Kim doesn't get much ice time with the Bantam A team. Apparently, Kim is afraid to go into the corners, and the rest of the guys on her team want her to quit. Shauna says they're mean to her. Huh, maybe that'll smarten her up.

"Kim, you might find that it's not so easy to play defence when you can't hit," Carla says quietly. "Don't take any unnecessary penalties, okay? You may not be serious about doing well in this tournament, but we are."

Whoa. If looks could kill, Carla would be dead.

At that moment, Mrs. Brewer comes in and surveys the dressing room. "Everyone ready for Coaches' Corner?" she asks.

Thank goodness it's time to go on the ice.

Despite the fact that the Regina Wolves appear to be bigger and faster, Steve is delighted with our roster. And Tara hits the crossbar twice during the warm-up – an excellent omen.

"The sky's the limit, girls!" Steve tells us in our huddle before game time. "Have fun out there!"

The Wolves have three forward lines and three sets of D. They look strong and fast. I'm happy to be back on a line with Tara and Amber. I like playing with Kathy, but she's very unpredictable, and she doesn't give me many pointers. On the other hand, Tara always tells me what I'm doing right and wrong, and I usually know where she's going to be on the ice.

More importantly as of twenty minutes ago, I want to ask Tara what's going on with Mark and Kim. If they're going out, why didn't she tell me?

Steve puts our line out for the opening faceoff. Kim and Carla back us up on defence. This is going to be tough, I think.

I have no idea how tough.

We quickly find ourselves in our own end, struggling to get the puck out. The three Wolves forwards are huge – as big as Carla. Thinking that Kim is in trouble, I go in deep to help clear the puck. Big mistake.

"Get back to the blue line!" Kim growls at me. "Play your position!"

I back off, and a few seconds later, the Wolves score.

I apologize to Tara as we skate back to the bench. "I just couldn't shake off that D-man."

"Try a little harder, next time, will ya?" Kim says as she skates past. "If you're tired, get off the ice!"

Once we're behind the boards, I whisper to Tara, "So what's with Kim and Mark?"

Tara looks irritated. "Get your head in the game."

Feeling foolish, I don't bring up Mark again.

By the middle of the second period — with the scoreboard showing 3-0 in favour of the Wolves — every muscle in my body aches and my legs feel like wet noodles.

Furthermore, it's getting harder and harder to keep my temper around Kim. She's always cutting me down.

"Hey, do something about that piano tied to your ass, will ya?" she shouts as I skate onto the ice for a faceoff in the Wolves' end.

I swear under my breath.

"I don't think Kim likes you much," Amber murmurs in my ear. "But don't worry. She's only with us for the weekend."

I sure hope so.

With six and a half minutes left, we get a break when Kathy forces the Wolves to take a holding penalty. Steve sends out our line for the power play. Thanks to some heads-up passing, we find ourselves set up in the Wolves' end, with Shauna and Jennifer lined up solidly on the blue line.

I am standing near the hash marks when the puck pops up to me. Out of the corner of my eye, I see that Shauna's open. I throw the puck back to her and she one-times a slapshot that clears the Regina zone like a cannon blast. The shot careens over the goalie's right shoulder, and the red light beams.

At last – our first goal!

"Nice shot!" Jennifer thumps Shauna on the back. "Great pass, Jessie!"

Tara grabs me by the cage and pulls my head close to her own. "Way to use the point man, Big Mac!"

"Dad's always telling me to do that – but I just never think of it in time," Amber sighs.

"We're in this game now, girls!" Shauna shouts as we head for the bench.

I look up into the stands where I know Mom and the rest of the parents are sitting. Mom is on her feet, cheering wildly and hugging Mrs. Howard, who is waving a white banner with "Xtreme" printed in black and yellow letters. The rest of the parents are shaking an assortment of noisemakers. Dr. Bilku is doing the Macarena. I wish Dad and Courtney could've been here to see my assist.

When we take our little skate past the box, I notice that Kim doesn't touch my glove.

Next time we're on the ice together, she says, "We're never gonna win this game with you cherry-picking at the blue line."

Now that totally deflates me.

"Am I a cherry picker?" I ask Tara the first chance I get.

Tara smacks me on the back. "Don't let her mess with your head, Jessie. You're doing great."

The goal pumps new life into our legs. A few minutes later, Larissa scores. The snowball keeps rolling, and after Tara makes a perfect pass, Amber scores her first goal of the season. We're all tied up going into the final period. On her first shift, Kim catches the Wolves napping. She splits the D and scores on her backhand, putting us ahead 4-3. It's a pretty nice goal I guess. Kim does have nice hands.

Still, Mr. Kowalski says Kim is struggling to adapt to the girls' game. Besides taking two penalties for body contact, she's got this habit of rushing the puck and then losing it when she gets sandwiched by the Wolves' defence.

"I'd like to see her play her position – just once," I say to Tara.

"Don't bash your teammates," she replies.

Mental note to self. Don't say anything more to Tara about Kim.

Both teams get chippy in the third, but few penalties are called. Even Kim seems to smarten up for a while.

Then, with seven minutes left, Kim gets into a scuffle in front of our net with a Regina winger twice her size. When the linesman steps in, Kim immediately starts beaking at him.

Luckily he doesn't give her a penalty. When Kim returns to the box, both our coaches try to give her some friendly advice, but she ignores them.

"Now that girl is what my dad would call 'high maintenance,'" Amber says.

On her next shift, Kim makes the mistake of riding a Wolves' forward into the boards once too often. She takes a checking-from-behind penalty and is tossed out of the game.

Aw, too bad, I think, watching her skate off the ice.

"I'm sure gonna miss her," Amber says, and then smiles innocently when she catches my eye.

"Don't be too smug, you guys," says Tara. "She'll have to sit out our next game too."

I try to feel badly about that, but somehow I just can't.

We burn ourselves out killing the penalty. At the two-minute mark, a Regina defenceman cheap-shots Larissa, crushing her against the boards, even though she doesn't have the puck. Larissa goes down in a heap.

No penalty is called against the Wolves.

We are outraged but keep our comments to ourselves. Steve hates it when players catcall the referee.

Slipping and sliding, Steve and Mr. Kowalski race across the ice towards Larissa. While they're bent over her, we have a little conference at the bench.

"That was a dirty hit." Miranda angrily tosses her empty water bottle into the box. "Any fool could see that."

"Who hit her?" Amber asks. "I wasn't looking, and I missed it."

Carla stares over at the Wolves' bench. "Number 11 – the one with the green Synergy."

Kathy says, "Someone needs to even the score."

It doesn't take a rocket scientist to guess that Kathy's going to be that someone. She has the same look on her face as she did that night at the Civic when she told Greasy Girl to go wash her hair.

After a few minutes, the coaches help Larissa to her feet and support her elbows as she skates weakly towards us. In response, both teams politely tap their sticks on the ice, but the Wolves look very smug.

I search for Doctor Bilku in the stands, but he's already made his way to the box. "Are you all right, Larissa?" he asks, white-lipped with fury.

Larissa nods bravely, but we can tell she is really shaken up.

"The refs can't see everything – so don't blame them," Steve says. "And Parker, don't take a stupid retaliation penalty with only two minutes left. We can win this game if we don't lose our heads."

Mr. Kowalski nods. "Kathy and Teneil should come off. Larissa, you should go to the dressing room."

Larissa shakes her head, then moans. "I need some Advil." She puts her head on her knees.

Doctor Bilku is already handing her some pills. "Larissa, you should listen to your coach."

Miranda says, "Don't worry, Larissa. We'll take care of her — one way or another."

"Get back to your net, Ebberts, before we get a delay of game," Steve growls.

Reluctantly, Miranda obeys. As I step out onto the ice with Tara and Amber, Kathy catches my arm and pulls me close.

"One lesson you need to learn about hockey — any kind of hockey," Kathy says, "is look out for your teammates. There's only two minutes left, and I may not get back on the ice again. You know what to do?"

I nod and step onto the ice, but deep down, I am terrified. Why me?

Then, as I take stock of my teammates, I understand. We need Tara on the ice at this point — and Amber is too small to do the job. Because there are only three of them, our defence can't afford to do anything about the dirty hit either.

As we line up at the faceoff dot just outside the Wolves' blue line, I look around to see if Number 11 is still on the ice. There she is, lined up across from Amber, with a cocky grin on her face. When the linesman drops the puck, the Wolves' centre wins the faceoff and draws back to her left defenceman, who passes ahead to Number 11.

I mumble a hasty prayer and skate straight across the ice at my target, who has just thrown the puck up to her centreman.

I have a full head of steam and don't let up. I even come off the ice a little as I drive my shoulder into her chest, slamming her against the boards. She drops like a stone, and the Regina bench erupts in shrieks of protest.

I skate straight for the penalty box and wait for the time-keeper to open the gate. I can already feel Steve's eyes boring two holes in the back of my jersey. None of the Xtreme dare cheer.

Assisted by two teammates, Number 11 skates to her bench. I note with great satisfaction — she isn't smiling now.

"Number 13 white. Two minutes for charging," the referee informs the scorekeeper.

I feel a little thrill of excitement. My first penalty. I finally risk a look at Steve, who is staring at the clock like a condemned man. My heart plummets to the pit of my stomach. What if I just cost us the game?

On pins and needles, I watch the dying seconds. Steve puts Tara, Kathy, Shauna, and Carla out for the penalty kill. As soon as the Wolves gain control of the puck, their goalie skates to the box, and with a little over a minute left, six Regina players take the ice against four Xtreme.

I feel a wave of pride as my four teammates block shot after shot and try to clear the zone. There are at least six face-offs in our end, but Miranda won't give an inch.

The Regina coach calls a time out with seven seconds left on the clock.

"I don't believe it," the timekeeper says. "Who would have thought a team from Estevan could beat us?"

As my teammates line up for the faceoff, I start to feel more confident. There's not enough time left for the Wolves to score two goals.

Before the horn sounds to end the game, Shauna ices the puck, scoring an empty-netter, and cements a 5–3 win for the Xtreme.

I fumble with the latch on the gate, eager to join in the celebration on the ice. Mom and the rest of the parents are going crazy in the stands. I leap into the throng of players swarming Miranda, throwing head-butts with the best of them.

"We did it!" Teneil throws an arm around my shoulders.

"We rock!" Kathy squeezes me until my ribs creak. "Awesome hit, Mac! That's what I call rough justice!"

As we line up to shake hands, the Wolves look like someone died.

"Regina sucks," I say happily, tapping Number 11's glove with my own. I hear her swearing all the rest of the way down the line, but I don't give a rip.

Afterwards Steve comes up behind me and says, "What was that hit all about, Mac?"

I turn slowly to face his dark blue gaze.

"That was stupid." He places his hands on my shoulders.

"You could have seriously injured that girl. Whatever possessed you to go after her like that?"

I lick my lips. "Somebody had to stand up for Larissa."

"Correction – nobody has to stand up for Larissa. She can take care of herself. I don't condone that kind of play, and I would never tell you to go after another player. It's bad enough that Parker goes off half-cocked once in a while. I don't need you following her lead."

I hang my head. "Sorry, Coach."

I don't know if he hears me because he's already heading toward the exit.

Later in the dressing room, while the Xtreme celebrate, I wrestle with my excitement and my guilt. It did feel good to level that girl – especially after what she did to Larissa – but it's not worth it if I have to live in the shadow of Steve's disappointment.

chapter fourteen

ack at the hotel, we push the limits of the coaches' eleven o'clock curfew. While the parents and coaches meet in the Langleys' room, we set up Party Central in the Kowalskis' and Brewers' adjoining rooms. Because Kim and her parents are staying with relatives across the city, I don't have to put up with Kim's smart remarks all night. We order in pizza and rent a movie. Then the fast pace of the game begins to catch up with us. Larissa goes to bed, complaining of a headache. In half an hour, most of the girls are snoring.

Kathy, Teneil and I stay awake and talk about all kinds of stuff. Eventually we end up discussing Kim. Although it sickens me to hear her name and Mark's connected, I don't try to change the topic, especially when it's obvious they don't like her any more than I do.

"Have you seen what's she's using for an MSN name?" Kathy asks us.

Teneil nods: "mark's-mine-so-hands-off. Can you believe it?"

Yeah, I can believe it.

"And what about her blogs on MySpace? You'd think she was the top scorer on the Bantam A team."

There's lots of talk about whether or not Kim will show at 8:00 tomorrow morning for our game against the Moose Jaw Panthers.

"Steve told her to come," says Teneil. "He'll be ticked if she doesn't."

"Steve's dreamin' if he thinks Kim's dad is going to drag himself out of bed tomorrow to come watch *girls* play hockey," Kathy says. "It isn't hard to tell where Kim gets her lousy attitude from."

Hmm, that's interesting. And here I thought she got it from her mom.

"Kind of makes me sick the way everyone sucks up to Kim." Teneil stifles a yawn.

I'd love to put in my two cents' worth, but I know better than to knock Kim in front of my teammates — not after the way Tara reacted tonight.

"Makes me sick too, but we need her," says Kathy.

"The Bruins have a game tomorrow at the Agridome." Teneil stretches and yawns again. "I'll bet she'll be watching."

"Do you think we can win without Kim?" I ask.

Kathy shakes her head. "But that checking-from-behind penalty at the end of the game really hurt. It's like Coach is always telling us — she must learn to use her natural aggressiveness for good — instead of evil!" she laughs.

"Good point," Teneil says. "You take dumb penalties all the time."

Kathy blushes. "So do you."

Definitely time to change the subject. "How about that Miranda in net? Wasn't she awesome tonight?"

It works. Pretty soon Kathy and Teneil are all friendly again.

Frankly, it won't break my heart if Kim doesn't show tomorrow. Then maybe Steve will quit tiptoeing around her and bench her in the evening game. If Kim and her dad go home in a huff, that'll be fine with me.

Everyone looks bleary-eyed when we arrive at the Northwest Arena at seven o'clock the next morning. My head feels fuzzy, and I wonder how I will ever suck up the energy to play three periods of hockey.

"I hope we have an easier game against Moose Jaw," Teneil says as we put on our equipment, which is damp and cold from Friday night's game. "Those Wolves were tough."

Tara smoothes back her hair. "So are the Sharks — if we get to play them."

"What do you mean – if?" I ask.

Kathy explains, "The Sharks are in the A pool, along with the Sabres and the Avonlea Lightning. If we win this morning, we'll play the second-place team in the A pool tonight."

"The Sharks beat Avonlea seven to zip last night." Amber rummages in her hockey bag and pulls out a sock. "They are definitely going to be a challenge."

"Well, let's just hope we get a chance to play them," Shauna says.

The door opens with a bang, and Kim walks in. You'd have to be blind not to notice how ticked she is.

"Morning, Kim," Tara says. "How'd you sleep last night?"

"Crappy!" Kim slumps on the bench next to Kathy and leans her head against the wall, folding her arms across her chest.

Her bad mood hangs like a heavy fog over our conversation for a few minutes. Eventually, Kathy brings her around by teasing her about Mark. It makes me want to puke.

"After your game, Dad's going to drive me over to the Agridome to watch Mark. Mark really wants me to be there," Kim says.

Thankfully, Shauna changes the subject. "What did you think about last night's game, Kim?"

Kim stands up and stretches. "It was okay," she says at last. "I didn't think girls' hockey would be that fast – or that rough. But the reffing's brutal." She continues, "You saw that checking-from-behind call I got. Dad says it was the worst call he's ever seen."

"Think you'd like to play some more games with us after the weekend?" Tara asks. "We could sure use another D-man."

Kim shrugs. "Dunno. Depends on the A team's schedule. I don't want to piss off my coach. "

Yeah, right. Teneil told us last night that Kim can't stand either of the Bantam A coaches. And Kathy thinks Kim would love to play with us all the time – except that she's shot off her mouth too many times about how lousy girls' hockey is.

"Did Steve say anything last night about provincials?" Kathy bites off a piece of sock tape. "Since we finally beat a Regina team, he's gotta think we have a shot."

"Yeah, Tara, what's Big Steve got to say about it?" Miranda asks.

"He'd like us to go." Tara ties her blue bandana at the back of her neck. "But he doesn't think we have enough depth."

"He's right." Shauna shakes her head. "Ten skaters and a goalie? That isn't enough. Players get hurt."

"If Randi came – and Kim – we'd be that much stronger," says Tara. "What do you say, Kim?"

Kim says, "I gotta think about it."

The door swings open and Mrs. Brewer enters, followed by Randi Hilderman, who wears a mile-wide grin.

"Is it true? Did you guys really beat a Regina team last night?" Randi throws down her equipment bag.

"She doesn't believe me." Mrs. Brewer smiles. "The Wolves' fans are also in a state of shock. Hurry up and get ready, girls."

Mrs. Brewer exits with a bang of the door.

"Believe it." Kathy drapes an arm over Randi's shoulder and tugs one of her auburn braids. "Now let Auntie Kathy tell you all about it."

The Panthers are no match for us, and we cruise to a 5-2 victory. The only wrinkle is Kathy loses an edge in the first period and plays lousy until she finds someone to sharpen her skate.

I enjoy beating the Moose Jaw team even though the game isn't as intense. We have now won our pool and have a berth in the semifinal, which is to be played at 6:00 Saturday evening.

"What would you girls like to do after we have breakfast?" asks Mrs. Howard as we head back to the hotel in her Suburban. "Shopping, swimming or sleeping?"

"The Midget Bruins are playing this afternoon at 1:30." Mom turns around and looks at both of us. "Maybe you girls would like to go watch."

My heart nearly stops. "Wouldn't you rather go shopping, Mom? You don't get to Regina very often."

"We can drop you girls off at the Agridome and go Christmas shopping. What if we pick you up around 4:30?"

"Sounds like you two are just trying to get rid of us." Teneil tries to peer into her mother's face by leaning as far forward as her seat belt will allow. "But we'll allow ourselves to be tricked — just this once."

"J ust who are the Bruins playing?" I ask Tara after we pay our admission and start walking towards the Agridome entrance.

"Swift Current," Tara replies. "I hope the refs are on their toes."

"Why do you say that?" I ask, buying a program from a man at the door.

"That Swift Current team is big — and they like to fight."

"Is Steve coming to watch?" asks Teneil.

"He and Mom are visiting some friends," replies Tara. "But he told me to tell you to watch and learn something about hockey — instead of just staring at the guys."

"As if we'd do that!" Teneil throws a sideways glance at Miranda. "And speaking of guys, I bet the view is better over there! Come on!"

She grabs Miranda's hand and the two of them bolt through the entrance, giggling. Just as we step through, a loud cheer goes up and Metallica's "Enter the Sandman" starts pounding.

Tara shouts, "Somebody must have scored already!"

I am surprised by the number of people at the game. This must be a pretty important tournament for the Midget Bruins. It feels great that I don't have to worry about Marsha and her pals being out there somewhere.

On the ice, five Swift Current players are gathered around their goalie, while the Bruins' line skates triumphantly past their bench.

"I'd say the Bruins have drawn first blood," Tara says.

I glance up at the clock — 19:21. It hasn't taken long for the Bruins to score. We start walking around the concourse, trying to decide where to sit.

"Tara!" A tall, blonde woman waves at us from a section of the stands off to our right.

Tara waves back and starts moving in her direction.

"Who's that?" I ask, as we make our way down the steps.

Tara grins. "My Aunt Maggie. Mark's mom."

I am still glowing crimson when Tara introduces me to Mrs. Taylor. It isn't hard to tell where Mark gets his good looks from.

"Jessie McIntyre," Mrs. Taylor says, after Tara has made the introductions. "Are you the girl who's having problems with kids from the Comp?"

I nod, speechless. It amazes me that so many people can know about my problems with Marsha — and my parents have never heard a thing.

"Did that girl ever get what she had coming?"

I shake my head. "It doesn't matter. They've left me alone."

"I don't know what that town is coming to," Mrs. Taylor says as the play on the ice resumes. "How'd your team do this morning?"

After Tara finishes her explanation, we find some seats several rows behind Mrs. Taylor. A few minutes later, Kim comes down the aisle, carrying two fountain drinks. She hands one to Mrs. Taylor and sits down next to her.

Tara stares at Kim for a while, then shakes her head.

"What are you thinking?" I ask.

"You know what I'm thinking," she replies, without looking at me.

I really don't, but I've learned not to criticize Kim in front of her.

When Mark steps on the ice, my eyes are glued to him, and when he's not, my attention keeps drifting back to Kim, who is keeping up a steady stream of conversation with Mrs. Taylor.

"Where's Mark's dad?" I ask after a while. "Doesn't he come to his games?"

Tara points to the other end of the arena, where a handful of spectators are standing at the rail. "He's over there. Auntie Maggie and Uncle Frank are divorced. He drove over from Calgary for the tournament."

I am shocked by this news, realizing there's a lot I don't know about Mark. "How long have they been divorced?" I ask.

"A few years."

By the end of the first period, the Bruins are leading 2-0. During the intermission, fans begin to move towards the concessions and washrooms. Kim stands up to stretch and notices us.

Rats.

She crawls over her seat and makes her way up the aisle.

"Great game, huh?" she says. "Mark's playing terrific D."

Tara and I both nod. I even manage a little smile, but I don't mean it.

"Tara, did you notice the Broncos are using the pick play?" Kim rests the arch of one foot on the back of a seat. "Remember the time in Lampman when I tried the same thing?"

Tara laughs. "That huge winger fell on top of you and neither of you could get up. You both just lay there waving your arms and legs. The two of you looked like a giant spider on its back."

"Yeah, he had his butt right in my face. I thought I was a goner for sure."

Kim sits down next to Tara and stays there for the rest of the intermission and the entire second period. She keeps up a steady stream of questions and autobiographical material, but she's only interested in talking to Tara, so it doesn't matter. I just watch the game, enjoying every minute that Mark's on the ice. One time he brings the puck all the way up the ice from behind his own net and scores.

"Who got that last goal?" Tara asks me.

"Mark did," I reply, surprised. "Didn't you see it?"

"Mark's quite the hot prospect," Kim says. "He'll be playing in the Dub next year."

"Where's that?" I ask.

"Don't you know anything about hockey?" Kim rolls her eyes.

"She means the WHL," Tara explains.

Kim adds, "I hear the Pats are interested in him."

Tara says, "He wants to graduate in Estevan. After that he plans to go out East to study engineering. He's not interested in a hockey career."

"I betcha he'll play with a WHL team if he has the chance," Kim says.

Tara looks at her long and hard and says, "You don't know him very well then."

Yeah, and I hope she doesn't get to know him any better.

At the end of the second period, the score is 4-2 for the Bruins. I credit the Bruins' comfortable lead to Mark's strong defence.

Tara stands up. "Let's go get something to drink, Jessie."

What a relief. I've had about all I can take of Kim for one day.

Kim walks down to sit with Mark's mom while we go look for an open concession booth. After we pay for our drinks, we find Shauna and her dad and watch the third period with them. The Bruins end up winning 5-4 and because it's not even four o'clock, Tara suggests we go to the lobby and wait for Mark to come out of the dressing room.

"What's the point?" I ask her. "Kim'll be there too."

"Don't you want to talk to Mark?" Tara responds.

I shake my head. Of course I want to, but like I told her, what's the point?

Against my better judgment, we go down to the lobby with the rest of the parents and fans to wait for the team. It takes a while of course. I feel like an idiot the whole time. Everyone except me has a reason to be there. Kim, who's still talking to Mark's mom, keeps giving me dirty looks. I just turn my back and ignore her.

Mark's dad comes over to talk to Tara, and she introduces me to him. He's about Mark's height, with silver hair.

"Jessie used to live in Saskatoon," Tara explains.

Mr. Taylor asks, "So how do you like living in Estevan?"

"It's okay," I reply. "I like playing hockey with the Xtreme."

"Well, you couldn't have found a nicer girl to hang out with." He gives Tara's arm a squeeze. "Not that I'm biased, of course. Now, how's your season going?"

Tara and I tell him about our games so far, and he tells us about the Calgary Flames. It turns out he's a season's ticket holder and a huge fan. He seems really nice. I wonder why he and Mark's mom split up.

Brian Smoltz is the first Bruin out of the dressing room. After he talks to Shauna for a while, they walk over to their dads.

Nathan's next, and he makes a beeline for Tara. She introduces him to her Uncle Frank, and they shake hands. Nathan's suit is a little small for him, and he hasn't quite got his tie on right, so Tara straightens it. Mr. Taylor starts teasing Nathan about Tara, and Nathan starts blushing. He doesn't say much — he never does say much — and all of a sudden it occurs to me why Tara wanted to hang around after the game. Why didn't she tell me she was going out with Nathan?

Miranda and Teneil join us, but they're so busy looking at all the other guys and whispering they hardly notice us. What a pair of flirts, I think to myself. But fortunately, they're harmless flirts.

Mark finally makes an appearance. His hair is still damp from the shower, and he's got it tucked behind his ears. He looks older wearing a suit and tie — and kind of funny without his baseball cap. He talks to his mom and Kim for a while, then joins our little group.

"Nice game, son." Mr. Taylor pats him on the back. "It was definitely worth the drive."

"Thanks, Dad," Mark says.

"Mark, do you know Jessie?" Mr. Taylor puts his hand on my shoulder.

Mark looks at me, but he doesn't smile. "We know each other."

I am so stupid. What am I doing here?

Mr. Taylor says, "The girls have just been telling me about their team. Sounds like girls' hockey is really taking off in Saskatchewan. I know it's big in Alberta."

That's when Kim butts between us. "The best female players always play boys' hockey first." She grabs Mark's arm and hangs on for dear life. This is one of those times I'd love to smack her. "Mark, you haven't introduced me to your dad," she says.

While Mark is making the introductions, Mr. Taylor's cellphone starts ringing. He apologizes, then pulls it out of his pocket and wanders off, deep in conversation. Kim looks thoroughly pissed off.

Tara excuses herself to go to the washroom, and Nathan walks over to Brian and Shauna. Now it's just me, Kim, and Mark — if you don't count Teneil and Miranda. I could actually talk to Mark about some important stuff if Kim would just butt out.

Small chance of that.

This other guy comes over, wearing a suit jacket and a toque, but no tie. He's about Mark's height, but heavier.

He grabs Mark by the arm and shakes him roughly. "Ready to go get some grub?" he says in a loud voice.

"Sure." Mark looks uncomfortable.

"Typical Mark," the new guy says. "If you wanna find him, just look for the ladies." He gives me a shark-toothed grin. "Haven't seen you before. You must be new to the harem."

I blush to the roots of my hair. I can't even stammer out a reply.

Mark introduces me to Greg Kolenick, one of the Bruin goalies.

"Actually, I'm the starter," he corrects Mark. "See that great kick save I made at the beginning of the second period, Jessie?"

Mark looks even unhappier, if that's possible. "We should be heading for the bus, Greg." He pats Kim's hand, then tries to pull away from her. "I'll talk to you later."

"Mark, when I first met you, I thought you were going out with Tara." It just pops out of my mouth before I can stop it. I have no idea where it came from.

Everyone looks at me like I've just accused Mark of being a pedophile. Even Teneil and Miranda stop talking for a minute and stare at me with these really wide eyes.

Crap! I better make this right. "Then I found out you're her cousin."

Kim starts laughing. She is so annoying.

Mark looks confused. "What are you talking about?"

"Jessie, you're even dumber than I thought!" Kim says.

I don't care if she tells the world how stupid I am. I just want Mark to know I don't think he's a scumbag.

Mark frowns at Kim. It makes me want to tell him a bunch more stuff, but I can't do it in front of everybody. I've already said enough as it is.

Greg slaps a big hand on Mark's shoulder and starts pulling him towards the arena entrance. "Let's go, buddy. Bus is waiting."

After the guys have left, Kim looks at me and says, "If you're trying to take Mark away from me, forget it."

I'd like to grab her by the throat and start squeezing. "That's not what I'm doing."

"Mark says you're a snob and a tease. So stay away from him." Kim walks back over to Mrs. Taylor and starts talking to her like there's nothing wrong.

I blink back the tears. I'm pretty sure Mark never said any such thing about me, but it still hurts.

"She is such a bag sometimes," Miranda says. "In fact, she's Super Bag."

That makes me feel a little better.

On our way back to the Northwest Arena for our game, I whisper to Tara, "What's Greg Kolenick like?"

She looks at me in horror. "You're not interested in him, are you?"

"Of course not," I say quickly. "I just got the impression he's a little stuck on himself."

"That's putting it mildly." Her mouth makes a grim line. "He used to go out with Kim, you know."

"Really?" I sit back to think. There wouldn't have been enough room in a relationship for both those egos. "I finally told Mark about the cousin thing," I tell her.

She gives me a long look. "Too bad you didn't suck up the courage weeks ago," she says. "You'd be a lot happier."

Don't I know that.

When we get to the arena, we put on some of our gear, then watch the Sharks play the Wolves for a while. Suddenly Tara realizes that we have only ten minutes left to get ready and we fly back to the dressing room, yanking on our equipment in record time. Kim won't even look at me. Suits me fine.

Once the game is underway, I have little time to think about Kim – or Mark. The Regina Sabres are a smaller team, but their forechecking is relentless.

Late in the first period with the score tied at 0, opportunity knocks when the Sabres take a roughing penalty.

"Who's still got legs?" Steve demands. "Shauna?"

Shauna, who has just come off a thirty-second shift, nods.

"Tara – you're centre. Kathy, take the off-wing. Jessie, go right. Kim and Shauna, you're D. Ladies, let's turn on the red light." He starts talking to Mr. Kowalski.

I hang back for a moment, wondering if he just made a mistake.

Steve looks up and sees me. "Are you trying to get us a delay of game? Get out there, Mac!"

My heart is racing as I skate to my spot inside the Sabres' blue line. Tara wins the puck back to Kim, whose slapshot rings off the post. The metallic clang rattles the Sabre defence, and they start scrambling.

I position myself in front of the net and lock eyes with the Sabre goalie. The D-man jams her stick between my legs and tries to push me out of the slot. Tara's behind the net, fighting two Sabres for the puck. She finally digs it out from the boards and throws it right on my blade. My first shot flies straight into the goalie's pads, but she gives up a juicy rebound, and I flick the puck into the open net on my backhand.

I feel an electrical charge of energy as the red light goes on, and I am mobbed by my linemates.

"I scored on my backhand!" I scream.

Tara throws her arms around me. "What a shot!"

"Now that's what I call a power play!" says Shauna.

Kathy smacks me on the helmet. "Way to go, Mac!"

Kim just says, "Didn't you hear me calling you? I had a clear shot from the point. You better learn to use your D man!"

You're just mad you didn't score, I think to myself.

The rest of the game is a hard-fought battle, but in the end, we earn a 1-0 victory, which gives us a berth in the A final on Sunday morning. I am dumbfounded when I get the medal for game MVP.

"Here, Miranda, you deserve this more than I do," I say later in the dressing room, laying the medal on the bench next to her helmet.

"I guess not!" Miranda stuffs the prize back into my hand. "You deserve it!"

"What's the plan for tonight, girls?" Amber asks. "Did Coach say we could go swimming?"

"Swimming's for kids," observes Kathy. "We want to party. Right, girls?"

And that's exactly what we do when we arrive back at the hotel after a team supper. Comfortably settled in Shauna's room with pop, munchies and a rental of *Mystery, Alaska,* we excitedly review the events of the past two days. All of us have discarded our dress code attire for T-shirts and sweatpants or pajama pants.

Sitting cross-legged on the bed while Teneil and Miranda try to put cornbraids in my hair, I can't remember feeling so content. I'm an MVP, and Kim is someplace far away.

Kathy, Jennifer and Larissa suddenly barge into the room and slam the door behind them.

"Quick! Hide us!" Kathy locks and bolts the door. "The security guard's on our tail!"

"First, tell us what you're up to." Shauna is reclining on the floor in front of the television. "We're not getting kicked out because of some stupid stunt of yours."

"We just threw some of those white plastic chairs in the pool!" Jennifer gasps.

"Excuse me, but isn't the pool area closed?" observes Tara.

"Yeah, that's why we had to throw them from the second floor balcony!" says Larissa. "The doors to the pool were locked!"

Kathy bangs on the bathroom door and Amber emerges, looking surprised. "Can't a girl have some privacy?" she asks, blinking her big blue eyes.

"Outta my way, Kowalski!" Kathy pushes Amber aside. "We need the shower!"

The three fugitives squeeze through the bathroom door and lock it behind them. We hear the shower curtain opening and closing and three girls giggling dementedly.

"Do you think anybody'll come here looking for them?" asks Carla.

A knock at the door answers that question.

"Okay, nobody panic." Shauna gets to her feet. "We never saw any girls, and we don't know anything about furniture in the pool."

We wait tensely while Shauna unlocks the door and admits the security guard — and Steve. I can see that Shauna is rattled. Lying to a security guard is one thing, but lying to Steve is another.

"Sorry to bother you, girls. The hotel has received some complaints about rowdy behaviour," Steve says. His piercing eyes search the room, clearly assessing the guilt or innocence of each pale face. "Where's Parker?"

"We haven't seen her," Randi says, a little too quickly.

Steve glares at Randi until she drops her gaze. "You're new to the Xtreme, Randi, so maybe you don't know about some of our team rules. Rule number one is don't lie to the coach. Now, where's Parker?"

Seven pairs of eyes swivel towards the bathroom.

Steve nods grimly. "Come on out, Parker! I know you're in there!"

There's an anxious silence, interrupted only by the hollow thunk of a shampoo bottle hitting the bottom of the bathtub. More giggles.

"Parker, I'm waiting! If you want to play in that final game tomorrow, you better get your fanny out here before I count to five. One... Two..."

The door is open before Steve can say, "Three," and Kathy, Jennifer and Larissa spill out of the bathroom.

"Don't count, Coach!" Kathy cries.

"You've got some cleanup to do down at the pool." Steve curtly gestures towards the hallway. "Get going. And be prepared to be bag skated at practice on Tuesday. I told you girls to behave yourselves at the hotel, and I meant it."

He's still scolding them when the door closes behind him.

We sit in stunned silence.

"Whoa," says Miranda, "am I glad he didn't catch me and Teneil dropping ice cubes on the people at the reservations desk!"

chapter
 fifteen

"I'm proud of you girls for getting this far," says Steve in the dressing room the following morning. "We've proved that there is girls' hockey in Estevan — and it's good hockey."

"It's great hockey!" shouts Kathy, pounding her stick on the rubber mat beneath her feet.

"That'll be proven by the outcome of this game, now, won't it?" Steve replies coolly. "And I'll thank you not to interrupt me, Parker."

"Sorry, Coach," Kathy says.

"Whether we win or lose, the Sharks are not going to forget that for the first time ever they are not playing another Regina team in the A final of this tournament." Steve pauses long enough to make sure every ear is listening. "Now, let's show them what an Estevan team can do."

One minute on the ice with the Regina Sharks — and we know we are outclassed. The Shark captain scores on her first shift, neatly undressing both Jennifer and Shauna in our end, and making Miranda look like a marble statue.

"That's okay!" Amber shouts from the bench. "We'll get it back!"

Embarrassed, the girls line up at center ice, but the Sharks' captain has no difficulty repeating the performance.

"This is going to be a long game," Mr. Kowalski sighs, staring at the clock.

On my first shift, I try to help Kim get the puck out of our end and fail dismally. She keeps sniping at me to play my position.

The Sharks score two more times.

I can't seem to do anything right. I'm always zigging when I should be zagging, and whenever I do get the puck, the Sharks are all over me like flies on manure. Even worse, Tara and Kathy can't move without someone hooking or holding them.

But the Sharks' best weapon is their goalie. She must be six feet tall and she can do the splits — both ways. If we do manage to get the puck past their blue line, nothing gets by her.

More bad luck halfway through period two. Tara catches an edge near the boards and goes down hard, smacking her head on the ice. Looking pale and shaken, she is escorted back to the dressing room and from there to the hospital for x-rays.

The loss of Tara at centre leaves a big hole – too big for Randi to fill. By the end of the second period, trailing by four goals, we are exhausted and frustrated.

On her first shift in the third period, there is one shining moment when Randi catches the Sharks' goaltender napping and scores on a shot from the red line. However, the Sharks reply with back-to-back goals, and the championship game ends 7–1 in favour of the Regina team.

Disheartened, we line up at centre ice to watch the Sharks' captain, who has scored four goals and assisted on two others, accept the first place trophy for her team and the Player of the Game award. However, we tap our sticks politely on the ice and shake hands with the A-side champions.

In the dressing room, Steve can't console us even when he tells us we played our best hockey ever in this tournament.

"Admit it, Coach." Kathy throws down her gloves. "We sucked."

"Pick up your bottom lip, Parker. You seem to be standing on it," Steve replies. "You girls just ran out of gas. You're not used to playing this many games in a weekend. And some of you might have broken curfew. Am I right?"

We look at one another shamefacedly.

"How's Tara doing?" asks Kim.

Steve runs a hand through his thick black hair. "Don't know. Her mother will call as soon as she knows anything."

"I hope she doesn't have a concussion," says Larissa. "That would be a bummer."

"We'd *never* beat another Regina team without Tara," says Amber.

Steve tries again. "I saw some great things on the ice this weekend, so don't be too hard on yourselves. You've shown me that we have a chance of winning a provincial final, and that's all I can ask of any team."

It's the first time Steve has ever mentioned the "P" word in the dressing room.

"Did you just say – provincials?" Kathy asks.

"Yes, I did." Steve smiles.

"The guys at school always say that girls' hockey sucks because there's no hitting," says Teneil. "Going to provincials would give us...would give us..."

"Credibility?" Steve suggests.

"Yeah, that," Teneil replies.

"Then go home and discuss it with your parents. We'll have a meeting after practice on Tuesday."

"Practice? Do we really need a practice, Coach?" Kathy leans her head against the cement wall and closes her eyes. "I think we got enough practice this weekend."

Steve's eyes flash. "Oh, we'll have that practice on Tuesday. Some of you girls need a reminder about how to conduct yourselves on the road. Now finish getting undressed. We have a team brunch at Smitty's in forty-five minutes."

I don't really understand why the mood in the dressing room is so much happier. I never went to provincials with my ringette team, so I don't know much about that level of competition. Since Tara isn't around, I don't want to ask any stupid questions. I ask enough of those as it is.

After Steve leaves, Shauna turns to Kathy and says, "Sounds like we're all gonna pay for that stunt of yours last night."

"I wasn't the only one!" Kathy blusters. "Remember, Larissa and Jennifer were in on it too, and Miranda said she and Teneil did some other stuff!"

"Everyone knows you're the ringleader, Kathy, and as a ringleader, you deserve a wedgie. What do you think, girls?" Shauna looks around the room for support.

Within seconds, Kathy is pinned on the floor beneath four or five players, screaming at the top of her lungs.

Carla and I watch calmly from the sidelines.

"Don't you love road trips?" Carla asks.

I grin back at her. "Sure do."

chapter
sixteen

ecause of her concussion, Tara misses practice on Tuesday night. She's lucky, because Steve lives up to his promise to bag skate us. Fortunately, he also cuts practice fifteen minutes short so he can meet with our parents to discuss the Female Bantam A Provincial Tournament in February. From the talk in the dressing room, it sounds like all the girls are eager to go.

"How many teams will there be at provincials?" I inquire.

"Steve thinks six or seven," Shauna says. "Regina and Saskatoon will each have a team there besides Rosetown, which is the host team."

"Which Regina team?" Larissa asks.

Shauna explains, "Regina and Saskatoon will have tryouts and pick an A team, taking the best players."

"Oh, great!" Kathy throws an elbow pad across the room. "As if we'd have a chance against an all-star team!"

"Hey, it's not as bad as it sounds," says Shauna. "Regina

and Saskatoon also pick AA teams, so their A teams will be made up of girls who weren't good enough to play in the AA tournament."

"So you're saying we won't be seeing the captain of the Sharks at provincials?" Larissa's eyes look hopeful.

Shauna nods and tosses Kathy her elbow pad. "That's exactly what I'm saying."

"If Kim and Randi come with us, we'd have a chance," Carla says. "We could also use two more forwards, so we'd have three lines. We don't have enough depth with nine players. And no offence, Miranda, but we need another goaltender. If you get hurt, we're done."

"I won't get hurt," Miranda says.

"I kind of like playing every second shift," says Teneil. "More players means less ice time for the rest of us."

"Carla's right. We're going to play four or five games in three days." Shauna jams her skates into her hockey bag and zips it shut. "We're going to need more players if we want to be competitive. Or...is it just about your ice time?"

Everyone looks at Shauna and falls silent.

Shauna takes a deep breath. "Competing at provincials isn't about goofing off, going swimming and ordering pizza. It's about representing our city. Steve should feel free to put his best players on the ice whenever he wants, and not have to worry about stepping on any of our feelings."

"What do you mean 'goofing off'?" Miranda demands. "I thought we played one hell of a tournament!"

"We wouldn't have done so well without Randi or Kim," Carla points out.

"I have no problem with Randi," Miranda says, pulling on her T-shirt. "And maybe Kim helped us, but when she took that checking-from-behind penalty, she nearly cost us a trip to the final."

"That's not fair," says Carla. "That could happen to anyone. Kim just needs some time to get used to playing girls' hockey."

"I don't see Kim here! But I come to every practice and game!" Jennifer's voice trembles with emotion. "What about the girls who are committed to this team all year?"

Murmurs of agreement greet this statement.

Shauna tries to mediate. "I'm just trying to say that we might have to make a few sacrifices to do what's best for the team."

Jennifer picks up her bag and hoists it over her shoulder. "Don't talk to me about sacrifice!" she shouts, tears welling in her eyes. "I gave up playing basketball this year to commit myself to hockey! Is Kim Scott that committed?"

"She cuts down girls' hockey every chance she gets!" Teneil says.

"Maybe this past weekend has changed her mind," Shauna replies.

"If I have to sit even one shift because of Kim Scott, then I might as well quit right now!" Jennifer grabs her sticks.

"Hey, Jennifer, don't talk like that," says Shauna. "I didn't mean to upset you."

Jennifer turns on her. "Did you miss any shifts in that game against the Sabres? No? Because I sure as hell did!"

She storms out of the dressing room. Shauna stands up and surveys the room, then follows her.

We sit in uncomfortable silence for a few moments.

Carla finally says, "Obviously I've said too much on the subject. Does anyone else want to try?"

Kathy says, "I'd rather sit a few shifts and win the tournament than play all the time and lose."

"It won't be you that's sitting," Larissa points out. "That's just the problem."

"This is all my fault." Carla stands up, shaking her head. "I keep forgetting that we're a house team."

"What's that supposed to mean?" Miranda asks.

Carla continues. "Let's face it. We barely have enough players as it is. If picking up other players is going to make people quit, then we shouldn't do it. We can take our regular team to provincials and with any luck we'll win a game or two."

Feeling confused, I roll up my shampoo bottle in my shower towel and stuff it into one of the side pouches of my equipment bag. For my own selfish reasons, I don't want Kim on our team any more than Jennifer does. I won't mind sitting on the bench for most of the tournament if it'll give Tara and Shauna a provincial championship, but I can't say the same about Kim. On the other hand, I don't want the other teams at the tournament to think our team sucks. What message will we be giving everyone if we go to provincials and get slaughtered?

As if reading my mind, Kathy says, "I don't wanna face the boys in my class if we get our asses handed to us at provincials. In fact, I'd rather not go at all."

I am beginning to realize just how hard it is to be a coach.

If we played the best hockey of our lives in Regina, we are at our worst on Friday night against the Southern Wildcats.

It's our last game before the Christmas break. With Tara watching from the sidelines, the Xtreme offence is pretty much non-existent. Even I have to admit that Kim doesn't play too badly, but Miranda has the most forgettable game of her hockey career. Jennifer refuses to come out of the dressing room in the third period, and Steve spends most of it trying to find out what's wrong. After three periods of – in Mr. Kowalski's words – "running around in our own end," we go down to defeat 8-2.

When we're dressed in our street clothes, Mrs. Brewer asks Randi and Kim to leave so we can have a team meeting. Steve and Mr. Kowalski come in, and Steve gives us this long lecture about dedication and self-sacrifice and commitment. Obviously Jennifer told him what happened after Tuesday's practice.

"Girls, the Wildcats will likely be the team we have to beat to advance to the provincial tournament," he says at last, and then asks helplessly, "should we just forget about provincials?"

"Do *you* want to go?" Kathy demands.

"Of course I want to go," Steve says. "I've waited four years to have a team that's strong enough."

"So you're saying that our team is strong enough now — without picking up other players?" asks Jennifer. We can all hear the tension in her voice.

"Yes, we're strong enough." Steve looks Jennifer right in the eye. "We can make a good showing there, but we probably won't win."

"Why do you want to go to provincials?" Jennifer asks.

Steve scratches his head and begins pacing. "Why do I want to go?" he says, more to himself than to us. He goes on pacing and muttering for a few seconds, then stops abruptly and looks at all of us. "I won't lie to you. Part of it is selfish. I was on a minor league team that won several provincial championships, and I also played junior hockey. I want Tara to have the experience of taking her game to a higher level. And that goes for the rest of you girls too."

"That doesn't sound selfish to me," Teneil says.

"Believe me, it's selfish. When you're a parent, you'll understand why." He takes a deep breath. "But most of all I'm sick to death of people not taking this sport seriously. I'm sick of the radio station not broadcasting your scores. I'm sick of having to beg for ice time so we can play three real periods of hockey. I'm sick of never playing a single game in the Civic Auditorium. I'm sick of not having a league to play in. Do you understand what I'm saying?"

We all nod. I've never heard Steve speak like this before.

"So let's pretend that we go to Rosetown and win the damn tournament," he says. "When we come back to Estevan, they'll honour you girls at a Bruins' game. They'll bring you all out on the ice and shake your hands – in front of every hockey fan in this city. They'll raise a provincial banner in the Civic and hang your team picture in the lobby. And no matter what happens in your life – no one will ever be able to take that away from you. No one." He pauses and adds quietly, "What do you think? Is that a good enough reason to go to Rosetown?"

Jennifer is crying by now. "I'm sorry, Coach," she says, her lower lip quivering. "I didn't know. I'm sorry."

Steve sits down next to her and puts an arm around her. "I wouldn't hurt any one of you girls for anything in the world," he says. "If competing at provincials is going to create bad feelings or cause rifts –"

"Don't say it, Coach," Larissa says. "We're big girls. We can handle sitting on the bench if you need us to."

"We trust you, Steve," Teneil says.

"Pick up a few more players – like Kim and Randi. We need more bodies," says Jennifer.

"And don't forget about signing another goalie," Miranda adds.

"Does everyone feel the same way?" he asks. "Do I need to talk to each of you privately?"

We shake our heads.

"Then I guess we're on our way to Rosetown." Steve rubs his big hands together. "I'll see you all after Christmas. Don't eat too much turkey."

chapter
seventeen

I t's a good thing that there's no hockey the last week before Christmas. Between Courtney's school concert, my parents' staff parties, housecleaning, baking and wrapping presents, our house is a busy place.

The night before the last day of school there's a formal dance at EJH. I don't really feel like going, but there seems to be a conspiracy to get me there — mainly because Kathy needs a "date." You see, our dances are normally closed to other schools, but this time, we get to bring a guest — as long as one of our parents comes as a chaperone. Naturally my dad has no difficulty agreeing, since he wants to spy on me all the time. He's always asking me if I need another can of "boy repellent."

Mom is more excited than the kids at school. She buys me this really cute skirt and top and makes an appointment to get my hair styled. When I come downstairs after getting ready, my dad's jaw nearly hits the floor.

"You look seventeen!" he says as he puts on his winter parka. "Are you sure that skirt meets dress code?"

"I'm sure," says Mom. "Have a nice time, Jessie."

We pick up Kathy, Miranda and Teneil at Teneil's house. My dad can't stop talking about how different we look. It's very embarrassing. After he parks the car, I quickly grab my backpack and hurry to the main entrance, hoping I can get inside long before he does. All I need is for him to say something in front of Mrs. Graham, the teacher in charge of the dance.

"Don't get upset, but I'm going to ask your dad to slow dance," says Kathy as we walk towards the gym entrance. "He looks hot tonight."

I knew I shouldn't have come. "Knock it off, will ya?"

After we sign in and pay our admission, Mrs. Graham tells us to go to the gym office and take off our coats. While I'm putting away my backpack, I realize that my medal is gone.

"What's wrong?" asks Kathy. "Did you forget something?"

"My Player of the Game medal from the Regina tournament! I hooked it to my backpack with a piece of wire – and now it's gone. It must've fallen off."

"That's too bad." Kathy puts a sympathetic hand on my shoulder. "But the way you play, you're gonna get another one sometime soon. Let's go find Shauna."

I feel like my whole night is ruined, but I follow her.

The disk jockey is seated on the stage, taking requests from a group of eager Grade Sevens. The music is so loud I can hardly think, and the light show isn't bad either. There are already two hundred kids here, which is a great turnout.

Shauna, who is standing near the back of the gym with Brian Smoltz, looks awesome. She's got her hair piled on her head in loose, tumbling curls, and she's wearing a flowered rayon skirt, blue tank top, and white lace blouse. She looks way too old to be at this dance.

Before long, Tara and Nathan arrive. I don't ask Tara if Mark is coming because I really don't want to know. I can't stand the thought of Kim wrapping around him like a snake during a slow dance. Every time I think about that night at the movie, I mentally kick myself about a thousand times. And why didn't I phone him afterward? I am such a loser.

I get to dance all the fast ones with the girls, since Nathan and Brian only know how to slow dance. When the DJ finally does play a few slow ones, Riley asks me to dance. I feel bad about dumping him the first week of school, and I tell him so. He says it doesn't matter. What a nice guy.

Afterward, I get some money out of my backpack and buy a pop from the machine. My dad is standing in the hall talking to Mrs. Graham and Mr. Kowalski. When they see me, they give me this guilty "Oops, you caught us talking about you" look. I don't really care because I know Mr. Kowalski likes me now, and I'm doing well in Mrs. Graham's math class; at least that's what she said at three-way conferences in November.

Mrs. Graham waves me over and pats me on the shoulder. "Jessie, I was just telling your dad how much higher your marks are in Term Two. If you keep up this pace, I'll consider you for the math award at the end of the year."

I just about faint from shock. "Really?"

"Really," she says.

"Way to go, kid." Dad looks proud enough to burst.

Wow. After I buy my pop, I go back into the gym and sit down on a chair along the sidelines, so I can take it in. I always was a good math student in elementary school, but I never had as many students to compete against. I make a mental note to start studying a little harder for algebra tests.

A female voice shouts in my ear, "What's up?"

I look up to see Kim leaning over me, taking a sip out of a Coke bottle. She's not very dressed up for a formal dance. She's got on a pair of beige cargo pants and a T-shirt. There's no sign of Natalie Wilgenbush – or Mark.

"Not much," I reply, determined to keep all answers to three words or less.

She starts talking to me about the hockey team, but I can't really hear her because the music's too loud. She suggests we go into the girls' washroom. I can't think of a single excuse, so I follow her across the gym. My heart starts beating faster. What's she up to?

Along the way, I make eye contact with Shauna, who is slow dancing with Brian. She looks concerned. Be careful, she mouths. At least she knows where I'm going.

Once inside the washroom, Kim flops down on one of the benches and pulls a silver flask out of the side pocket of her cargo jeans. Oh man, this is trouble. She takes a quick glance at the stalls to make sure none of them are occupied.

I try to think of an excuse to leave, but my mind draws a blank.

Kim pours the contents of the flask into her Coke bottle, then returns the flask to her pocket.

"What's a school dance without some booze?" She takes a swallow, wipes her mouth, and holds out the bottle.

"No thanks."

"Are you sure?" She wiggles the bottle temptingly.

When I shake my head, she takes another sip. I look at the door and mentally will someone to come in – preferably not a teacher. Any excuse to end this conversation.

"Look Jessie, I really do want to play hockey with you guys whenever I can fit it in. You're a fun team."

"Thanks."

"It's just that my first commitment is to the guys, you know?"

Whatever. We all know the guys on her team want her to quit. Teneil says they tell her she sucks right to her face. How can she stand it?

I decide a change of subject is necessary. "Why didn't you bring Mark to the dance?"

A little shadow of pain crosses her face. I have definitely struck a nerve.

"He couldn't come," she says. "He's studying for SATs."

If he really liked Kim, he'd be here.

She takes another sip. "Are you sure you don't want a drink?"

Two Grade Seven girls open the bathroom door and enter, giggling.

Perfect. I stand up and back towards the door. "I gotta find Kathy."

Kim leans back against the brick wall and stretches out her legs. "Been nice talking to you, Jessie. Maybe we can do this again sometime."

I leave the washroom and go looking for Kathy. After all she is my date, and a person just can't set Kathy down in the middle of two hundred people and forget about her for very long. She has a habit of stirring things up.

Kim's dad comes and takes her home before long. Good for him. The last thing I need is her getting into trouble for bringing alcohol to school and dragging me down with her.

Anyway, I have a pretty good time for the rest of the dance – in spite of the fact Shauna and Kathy want to hear all the details about what happened in the washroom. I tell them I don't feel like talking about it – especially not when Natalie Wilgenbush is sure to be lurking around a corner, waiting for me to start bashing Kim again. Fortunately, Riley asks me to dance, and that's the end of the interrogation. I end up dancing with him and talking to him for the rest of the night.

The DJ plays two slow dances right at the end, just when we're all damp and sticky. One of the chaperones opens the back doors of the gym to let in some fresh air, and we're enveloped in clouds of mist.

As the final Aerosmith tune ends, everyone starts chanting, "One more song! One more song!" but Mrs. Graham throws on the gym lights. The long fluorescents flicker on right away, but the round ones crackle and sputter for at least five minutes before firing up. The teachers are already sweeping the floor, and they've even managed to put away most of the chairs. I think they play those slow ones at the end on purpose, knowing we'll all try to get in one more sweaty snuggle before the night is over.

There's a crowd of parents standing near the pop machine, waiting to take their kids home, so the gym empties out quickly. My dad rounds up me and Teneil and Miranda and – of course – Kathy, who's trying to shake free of some little red-headed twerp in Grade Seven. Teneil and Miranda think it's hilarious, of course. I'm just glad to have some artillery to use on Kathy for the times she teases me about my dad. Riley keeps hanging around on the fringe, like he wants to talk to me or something.

Thankfully he keeps his distance until after my dad goes outside to warm up the Explorer and scrape the windshield. I guess we had some freezing rain while the dance was going on, and the roads and sidewalks are really slippery.

Then Riley sidles up to me and asks if I want to go to a show with him after the Christmas break.

"I'd like to go sooner," he tells me, "but I'm going to my grandparents' farm for the holidays, and after that we're going skiing in Montana."

I tell him that I will, but my heart isn't in it. I still like Mark, even though Mark clearly isn't interested in me. I'm not so sure he's interested in Kim either — or else he'd have come to the dance.

What would a guy like Mark want with a girlfriend in Grade Nine anyway? Especially when he has his pick of girls at the Comp.

After the four of us get our coats and backpacks, we grab hands and venture out onto the sidewalk. It's like a sheet of ice. Too bad we don't have our skates. We slip and slide like Bambi and Thumper all the way to the parking lot, giggling and screaming the whole way.

Because of the bright headlights and billowing exhaust fumes, I don't notice Rick's Camaro until I'm right in front of it. My heart freezes for an instant, and then starts jackhammering like crazy. Kathy's hand tightens on my arm, so I know she's seen the car too.

Marsha's leaning against the passenger door of the Camaro, her arms folded on the hood. Through the car's windshield, I can see Rick's face. There are more heads in the back seat, but I can't tell who they belong to.

"Come here, rich girl," Marsha says, jerking her chin in my direction. "I wanna talk to you."

Crap! Where's my dad?

Before I can say anything, Kathy speaks up. "You're lucky I'm wearing this skirt, or I'd come right over there and kick your ass."

Marsha shoots Kathy a killing look. "I wasn't talking to you!"

Miranda chooses that moment to lose her balance and fall right on her own ass, pulling all three of us down on top of her.

"Sorry, guys!"

"Ouch, who's got their elbow in my eye!"

"I think I ripped my skirt!"

It's like a scene out of a Spice Girls movie.

Marsha steps away from the car and stands over us, while we struggle to our feet. Teneil falls down two more times before she makes it up.

"Tell your friends to get lost for a minute," Marsha says to me. She doesn't sound angry, just annoyed.

"What about your friends?" Kathy jerks her head at the Camaro.

"For the last time, I'm not talking to you!" Marsha glares at Kathy.

Frankly, I'm surprised Marsha hasn't sworn yet. Compared to Halloween night, she's a real kitten.

Dad pulls up in the Explorer. The windshield is scraped free of ice, but there's no way he can see us through the passenger window.

"That's our ride." I grab Kathy's hand and start negotiating the icy sidewalk that runs along the perimeter of the parking lot. "See you round, Marsha." I really hope I won't.

We climb into the SUV, which is quite a few degrees warmer than the chilly air outside. Marsha just stands there, staring at us.

"I can't believe she never swore at us — not even once," Kathy says.

"Who?" Dad asks.

"Just one of Kathy's friends from the Comp," I say quickly, silently willing the other girls to keep their mouths shut.

As we pull away from the curb, Kathy rolls down the rear passenger window and leans out, singing, "We Wish You a

Merry Christmas!" Her voice is considerably worse than mine.

Miranda and Teneil start laughing.

Kathy sits back down and pushes the switch to raise the window. She grins at us and says, "Yep, she's swearin' now."

Later that night, I lie in bed, staring at the poster of the Canadian Women's Olympic Team, and think about how unhappy Kim looked, sprawled on that bench with that bottle in her hand. Is that what's eating her? She's unhappy? And am I the only one who knows just how unhappy she is? Well, she's too proud to admit that she's over her head playing A hockey — at least on that team. And Tara says some of those boys have a serious chip on their shoulder because they didn't make the AA team, and Jodi did, so they're taking it out on Kim.

"Kim's a good hockey player," Shauna told me one time on MSN, "but she got run a couple of times at the beginning of the season. She's lost her confidence. "

And then there's Mark. Kim tells everybody that she's going out with him, but it's obvious he doesn't like her nearly as much as she likes him. Tara says he never talks about Kim. Heck, he even tells Tara to mind her own business if she mentions her.

And Marsha. I guess it was stupid to think she might have forgotten about me. And in only eight months, I'll be a student at ECS – on her turf. How am I ever going to avoid her there? I can only hope she'll get herself expelled.

My mom knocks on my door and opens it a crack. "How come you still have your light on, Jessie? Can't you sleep?"

"No."

"Did something happen at the dance?" Mom walks into the room and sits down on the edge of my bed.

I tell her about Kim – not everything of course. She'd flip if she knew everything.

After I'm finished, Mom clears her throat. "I see. Did you tell Mrs. Graham about the alcohol?"

Trust a parent to miss the point entirely. "Of course not! Do you think I'm stupid?"

After a long silence, Mom says, "Was Kim trying to apologize?"

"Dunno." I wish I did know. Was she looking for sympathy maybe? Or just trying to get me drunk so I'd get into trouble again?

"Why don't you sleep on it?" Mom stands up and flips the light switch. "See you in the morning."

When Mom leaves, I fold my arms behind my head and stare at the ceiling. It's a long time before I fall asleep.

chapter eighteen

ecember 24th sets a provincial record for the warmest Christmas Eve ever in Saskatchewan. There isn't a flake of snow anywhere, and the mercury soars to a record eight degrees Celsius. Courtney and I grab our softball mitts and play catch before supper. After the Christmas Eve service, we come home to open one gift and enjoy some eggnog by the fire – the first time the fireplace has been used all winter. Dad thinks it's already too warm in the house, but Mom insists.

"It's not Christmas without a fire." She tosses another log on the grate. Courtney wastes no time dragging out the largest present from under the tree and tearing at the colourful wrapping paper like a hungry scavenger. Underneath, she discovers a new Barbie house.

Courtney hugs Mom. "It's just what I wanted!"

"Thank your father." Mom returns the hug. "He's the one who decided not to spare a penny this year."

"Why don't you open one of yours, Jessie?" Dad asks after Courtney has thanked him too.

I look uncertainly at the tree. "I don't know which one to open."

Dad squeezes my knee and points to an enormous box wrapped in gold foil. "Why not try that one?"

With some difficulty, I drag the package from behind the tree and pull it into the centre of the room. Stripping off the wrapping paper, I find a plain cardboard box underneath.

"Keep going, Jessie," Mom urges.

I peel the masking tape off the lid and look inside.

"Holy cow!"

"If any of it isn't the right size, we can exchange it," says Dad.

I pull out a pair of hockey pants, shoulder pads, elbow pads, shin pads, and a new helmet.

I look at my parents in amazement. "You didn't have to do this! My old equipment would have lasted me the winter."

"Just remember – most of it was begged, borrowed or stolen from our neighbours. We have to return it eventually." Dad hands me an envelope. "You'll need this too."

"Shouldn't I open it tomorrow?" I ask.

"Yes!" Courtney states emphatically.

"I think we can make an exception in this case, Princess." Dad picks up one of the elbow pads and straps it on his own arm. "Go ahead, Jessie."

I tear apart the envelope and open the Christmas card, which contains a gift certificate for a local sporting goods store.

"That should cover the cost of some new skates, shouldn't it?" Mom asks.

I hug each of my parents. "Thanks. But I don't deserve it."

"Of course you do." Mom smiles. "Any girl who has as much fun as you do deserves to have her own equipment." She passes Dad a plate of shortbread cookies.

"Your mom could hardly stand keeping it a secret," Dad says, taking a cookie. "She even put it on herself a few times."

"I'd like to have seen that!" I start laughing.

Mom puts her hands on her hips. "Never mind. By the way, Jessie, Mr. Kowalski called earlier today and said you're playing Melita on the 27th."

"Really?" I can hardly wait to try out my new gear.

"The Brewers will be gone, so he asked me to help coach." Dad helps himself to another cookie.

I shoot him a desperate glance. I can just picture Kathy and Teneil making cow eyes at Dad behind his back. This "hot dad" thing is really embarrassing.

"I'm kidding." Dad grins. "Mr. Scott is going to help coach."

Now that should be entertaining. Tara says Kim's dad coaches her brother's hockey team and makes an ass of himself every time he steps on the ice.

Oh well, better Kim's dad than mine.

When I walk into the dressing room two days later, the girls are even more excited and talkative than usual. We haven't been together for a while, and even though we've kept in touch on MSN there's still lots to catch up on. Apparently Kathy got her belly button pierced – a present from her mom – but her dad doesn't know about it yet, so it's very hush-hush. Everyone's teasing each other about who got the best Christmas present, who's the most spoiled, and who's got the richest parents. The honour falls to Miranda this time, since she's on holidays in the Dominican Republic with her family and unable to defend herself. Tara is also missing, but Kim and Randi are there and a girl with short, blonde hair that I've never seen before.

"This is Crystal Jordan," Shauna explains. "She's been playing Peewee boys hockey in Torquay, but she's thinking about going to Rosetown with us."

"What position?" I ask.

Kim points to Crystal's equipment and sneers at me. "Didn't you notice the goalie pads?"

Give it a rest already, Sourpuss. I knew that performance in the bathroom during the Christmas dance was just an act.

"I'm just backing up Miranda. I don't expect to play," Crystal says quickly. I can tell that she's nervous.

"Welcome to the Xtreme, Crystal." I stand up and formally shake her hand.

As I sit down again, Shauna gives me a nod of approval.

When I open my hockey bag and start pulling out my equipment, I quickly become the new target.

"What's with all the fancy gear?" Kathy holds up one of my gloves and whistles appreciatively. "Somebody sure likes you!"

Jennifer jabs me in the ribs with her elbow. "Guess Santa thought you were a good little girl this year. Too bad he never talked to any of us!"

"Like to snag me a rich guy like Jessie's dad," says Kathy, looking sly.

Oh, great. Here we go again.

"Think you'd like to have me for a stepmom?" she asks.

I throw a hip check and knock her off the end of the bench.

When we're ready, Mr. Kowalski comes in, followed by a short, stocky man wearing a sour expression. Hmm, with a look like that, he's gotta be Kim's dad.

"Everyone have a good Christmas?" Mr. Kowalski asks good-naturedly as he removes a few cards from his clipboard. He doesn't wait for a reply. "Most of you know the Brewers are away for a few days. Mr. Scott has kindly agreed to help run the defence for today's game. "

"Somebody who knows something," Kim mutters under her breath.

That figures. She'd no doubt like her dad to take over the whole team.

Mr. Kowalski continues. "Before you leave today, I need each of you to fill out one of these cards." He starts handing them out.

"What are they, Coach?" Teneil asks.

"Provincial cards," he replies, smiling.

"But those ones are already filled out." Larissa is sitting close enough to Mr. Kowalski to see a little of the writing. "Who do they belong to?"

He clips them back on his board before replying. "Kim and – Jodi Palmer."

There is an audible intake of breath.

"Jodi Palmer's coming with us to Rosetown!" Kathy gasps. "No way!"

"Yes, way," says Mr. Kowalski. "Does anybody have a problem with that?"

We all look at one another. From Shauna's expression, I can tell she already knew. Carla doesn't look very surprised either. Kim looks totally pissed off.

I'm confused. "I thought Jodi broke her collarbone. Will she be able to play by February?"

"Good question," Mr. Scott says gruffly.

"Her doctor told her that she should be on the ice by the end of January. That gives her two weeks to get her legs back," Mr. Kowalski explains.

Teneil asks, "Doesn't she want to go to provincials with the AA team?"

Mr. Kowalski says, "Her parents don't think it's safe for her to go into playoffs with the AA team so soon after her injury heals."

"What about Randi? Is she coming with us too?" asks Kathy.

Mr. Kowalski nods. "I know it means we'll have to juggle lines, but we can't afford to turn away any quality players — not with our short bench." He pauses to let the impact of this statement sink in. "So nobody gets hurt between now and February 20th, okay?"

"We're going to kick some serious butt in Rosetown," Kathy says confidently.

"Stifle yourself, Parker. We're not there yet," Mr. Kowalski replies, sounding just like Steve. "And we may have to play off against another team to qualify. Speaking of that, do you think you girls could play a little better than you did against the Wildcats last time?"

On our way out to the ice, I find myself sandwiched between Shauna and Carla.

"How's the new equipment feel?" asks Shauna.

"Like cement. I don't think I'm going to have much of a game."

"Well, you look great — if that's any consolation," says Carla. "It's about time you got rid of that blue CCM helmet."

"Hey, I liked that helmet!" I smack her lightly on the shoulder. "And what's with Kim's dad coming on the bench? Does Steve know about this?"

"Probably not," Shauna responds, shaking her head. "Amber says he invited himself, and Mr. Kowalski didn't have the nerve to tell him to stay out."

"Kim didn't seem too thrilled with the idea," Carla murmurs.

"Yeah, that was my impression too." I look over my shoulder at the coaches. "Tara says he likes to yell."

"If he's going to yell, I hope he has something important to yell about," says Shauna.

The Melita Raiders have brought three full lines and a group of enthusiastic parents and grandparents. This turns out to be one of the better-attended games we have played in the LMC.

Throughout the entire warm-up, I feel as if I'm wearing a suit of armour. Nothing bends right, and my skates are pinching my ankles. However, I'm not too miserable to notice how well Crystal moves in net. She's not very tall, but she has a great glove hand and quick feet. I sure hope she comes to Rosetown.

From the moment I step on the ice for my first shift, I always seem to be out of the play. Twice in the corner, the Raider defenceman beats me to the puck and gets body position on me. Mr. Kowalski doesn't say anything for a while, but when I come in after my third shift, he pulls me aside. "What's wrong, Jessie? Too much turkey?"

I shake my head in frustration. "It's this new equipment. I can hardly move!"

He nods sympathetically. "You'll just have to break it in."

"Did you tell her to get off her lazy ass?" Mr. Scott shouts from the other end of the bench. "Maybe she'd like to sit off her next shift!"

What a loser! Is Kim paying him to say that?

"What's with that guy?" Amber moans. "Does he think this is the Olympics?"

Midway through the first period, Kim rushes the puck and scores by going upstairs on the goalie's glove side. A nice goal – no matter who scored it.

"Awesome, Kim!" Mr. Scott shouts, raising his hands and clapping them above his head. "That's the way! You show these girls how it's done!"

"Don't say anything," Mr. Kowalski says, looking straight ahead. "Just pretend he's not there."

"This is one time I'm glad we're not playing stop time," says Kathy.

Steve would probably be happy with the way we play, seeing as we've been off the ice for two weeks. But Mr. Scott makes no secret of the fact that he thinks we're lousy.

"You call yourself a hockey player?" he shouts at Teneil when she fails to score on a breakaway. "With a weak-assed shot like that, you should be playing croquet!"

At first we are all annoyed by his constant ranting and arm waving. Then in the second period when his face turns purple and this big vein in his temple starts throbbing, we start to fear for his life.

"He's going to have a heart attack," says Larissa, "and my dad isn't here! What happens if he keels over in the middle of the game?"

By the third period we are all wishing he would.

We end up winning the game 5-2. Kim has three points, and Kathy has four, so Mr. Scott is delighted with their performance. He doesn't care about the fact that Kim left Crystal high and dry on one of Melita's goals because she was running all over the ice. Mr. Scott is so different from Steve, it's amazing. Steve is happiest when we play our positions well and beat the other team to the puck. As long as we do that, he says that the points will take care of themselves.

I'm in a foul mood when I step off the ice. My ankles are rubbed raw, and my arms are chafed from the chemical preservative used in my new elbow pads.

Outside the dressing room, Marsha is waiting for me. Damn, I'm too tired to take her on. She looks tough with that purple stud in her nose and that woolen toque pulled down over her ears and the rings through her lower lip and eye-brow. As soon as she opens her mouth, I realize her nose stud isn't the only new piercing.

The ball in Marsha's tongue clicks against her teeth. "Haven't seen you around for a long time. Been hiding?"

"Not really." And the truth is – I *haven't* been hiding. I haven't even thought of Marsha once in the past few weeks.

"Look, Jessie, I've been trying to talk to you forever," she says.

It's the first time she's ever called me by name. I pull off my helmet and shake my head, sending droplets of sweat flying. If I have to, I can clobber her with my helmet.

Marsha flicks a drop of sweat off her cheek. "I need a favour from you."

Whoa. I didn't see that one coming.

Marsha heaves a sigh. I can tell this isn't easy for her. "I need you to put in a good word with Brewer. He's been all over me like a rash for weeks. He says he's got enough on me to send me to Dojack for a year. You gotta tell him I'm leaving you alone."

My mouth falls open. No wonder she hasn't threatened me since that night outside the Civic. Maybe she's actually been wanting to tell me this all along.

Marsha says impatiently, "Look, I've got better things to do than stand here looking at your frickin' tonsils. Are you going to talk to Brewer or not?"

"I'll tell him — as soon as he gets back from holidays."

"Thanks. No hard feelings, huh?"

"There are plenty of hard feelings, Marsha. Just stay away from me."

"No problem." Marsha turns on her heel and walks away.

The wave of relief hits two minutes later in the dressing room as I strip off my sweat-soaked equipment. Does this mean I won't have to worry about Marsha when I go to ECS next fall?

Kathy saw me talking to Marsha and wants to know what's going on. After I finish telling her, she says, "That's great, Jessie, but just remember, if you ever need Auntie Kathy, she's got your back."

When we're finally dressed in our street clothes, Mr. Kowalski comes in to pick up the provincial cards. We're relieved to see that Mr. Scott is not trailing behind him.

"Will we take a bus to Rosetown, Coach?" asks Kathy.

"A bus? What do you think we are, Parker — an AA team?" he responds, laughing.

"The A team always takes a bus," Kim says.

Mr. Kowalski gives Kim a look of annoyance and then declares, "Of course we'll take a bus — as long as we can fill it with players and fans."

When I hand him my card, he asks me to hang around a minute so he can talk to me.

"Sure, Coach." Wondering what he wants, I step out into the hallway to wait.

Mark Taylor and Brian Smoltz are standing about three metres away talking to Shauna's mom, a short, plump woman who looks old enough to be Shauna's grandmother.

Oh, great. If I'd known Mark was watching, I would've stayed in the dressing room.

"Hi, Jessie!" Mrs. Langley smiles and waves. "Is Shauna just about ready? We're having a family dinner, and we should have left ten minutes ago."

At that moment, Shauna walks out, nearly knocking me over with her equipment bag. "Sorry, Jessie! Gotta run!" She breezes past her mother and grabs Brian's arm, dragging him along. "Come on, Mom! What are you waiting for?"

Mrs. Langley gives me a helpless look and follows in Shauna's wake, leaving Mark and me alone for the first time in weeks.

"How are you doing, Jessie?" Mark asks, shoving his hands in the pockets of his black windbreaker.

"Fine, I guess." I curse myself for not thinking of a dazzling reply.

"You played well today."

"Thanks." What I'd really like to say is, sorry for acting like a jerk.

"Tara says you're going to Rosetown for provincials in February."

"We have to knock out the Wildcats first." Actually, you're the nicest and cutest guy I've ever met.

"Right. What's your record against them?"

"Two losses." On the other hand, I'm the biggest loser on the face of the earth.

"Well, you're due to beat them then."

"I guess so." So now that you know how I really feel, can we just start over again? Yeah, fat chance of that.

One by one the girls leave the dressing room, and the steady stream of interruptions allows us no opportunity to talk of anything else. Inside my head, I am screaming with frustration.

Then Kim walks out. The range of emotions that race across her face in two seconds is amazing — surprise, alarm, suspicion, jealousy. She could win an Academy Award except I know that she's not acting.

"Let's go, Mark," she says, marching past us. "Dad's waiting."

"See you around, Jessie," Mark says. He gives me this wistful smile and turns the corner.

At that moment, Mr. Kowalski sticks his head out the door. "Ready to see me now?" he asks.

"Sure." I step inside. The humid air is stifling.

"Now that Jodi has agreed to play with us in Rosetown, Steve and I are thinking of making a few changes. Just how well are you getting along with Kim these days?"

I have no idea where this is leading. I open my mouth to tell him the truth, and then reconsider. Just before Christmas, we all agreed to uphold the coaches' decisions. Am I going to wriggle out from under that promise, just because a decision affects me directly?

"Much better, Coach. I think she's finally starting to like me."

"Great. I'll keep you posted."

When I leave the room a second time, I figure I'm the one who deserves the award for best actress.

chapter
nineteen

January flies by. We finally get a couple of feet of snow, so it actually feels and looks like winter. We end up having a few games cancelled and postponed because of bad roads. However, we do win one-day tournaments in Melita and Weyburn and then lose by one goal to a tough Medicine Hat team in the A-final at the Moose Jaw tournament. Steve thinks we're going to peak at just the right time for provincials.

Jodi Palmer plays with us in Moose Jaw and makes a huge difference to our team. I love Jodi's grittiness and stamina. She can accelerate from a standstill to top speed in seconds. She works hard in the corners and is relentless around the net. She never complains about her collarbone or disses girls' hockey. And after five minutes in our dressing room, she fits like a glove. She likes to tease us, but she does it in such a nice way, that we can't help liking her.

In short, Jodi Palmer is the exact opposite of Kim Scott.

And that's where things get really interesting. It's obvious to everyone — except maybe to Jodi — that Kim can't stand her.

On the personal side of things, I start going out with Riley again. He's so nice to me that I wonder why I ever dumped him in the first place. I guess it's because I never took the time to get to know him. My mom and dad like Riley because he's my age and he's so polite around them. He calls them Mr. and Mrs. McIntyre, and always talks to them about city politics and snow removal and stuff like that.

Before I know it, it's February.

Jodi Palmer has a party at her place one weekend when the Midget Bruins are playing at home. She lives on a farm west of Macoun, so Riley and I have to hitch a ride with Tara and Nathan after the Midgets beat Weyburn 2-1. Naturally my dad wants to check out Nathan first, but he comes around when he realizes that Nathan must be all right if he's dating an RCMP officer's daughter.

By the time we get to Macoun, it's after eleven.

"Doesn't your coach have a curfew?" I ask Nathan.

Nathan shrugs. "Let me worry about that."

Tons of vehicles are parked in the snowbanks along Jodi's lane. Good thing my parents can't see this.

"The Bantam AA team's playing at home too," Tara says. "I'm sure Jodi's invited them all."

As soon as we get inside, we take off our shoes. Jodi has a really nice house, but that isn't what makes an impression. Rap music is booming in the living room, dining room, and kitchen, which are packed with kids drinking beer. Nearly everybody's wearing a team jacket of some kind. It doesn't look like Marsha's here. It isn't really her kind of crowd — except maybe the kids in the solarium shotgunning. Well, she can shotgun all the beer she wants as long as she stays away from me — and since I told Steve that's what she's been doing, I can pretty much forget about her. Which suits me fine.

The front door opens and two boys walk in. I have no idea who they are, and Riley and Nathan don't seem to know them either. They smile at us in a friendly way and say, "How's it going?" but their eyes look kind of funny.

As they walk by us, I catch a whiff of weed and exchange panicked glances with Riley. "Aren't Jodi's parents home?" I whisper to him.

Riley's eyes are huge. "It doesn't look like it."

I want to tell Nathan my parents would crap bricks if they saw what's going on, but I don't dare. It's taken me six months to get out of Estevan on a Friday night, and I don't want to screw up now.

"Wanna beer?" Riley says.

I am too anxious to refuse. After he gets our drinks, we go down to the basement and watch part of the skills competition for the NHL All-Star game. It's an exciting place to be because every guy and girl in the room knows a hundred times more about these players than they do about chemistry, history or calculus. Riley, who plays house hockey, is just as absorbed as the rest of them.

Mark is sitting on the couch across the room from me with Kim snuggled under his arm. She keeps looking at me and smiling. I'd like to slap her face and scream, "Knock it off already! You've won, okay! You don't have to keep rubbing it in!" I have to force myself to listen to Riley and not stare at Mark like some lovesick cow.

After half an hour, I get up to use the washroom. I don't really have to go. I just want to get rid of the half bottle of warm beer I'm holding. I pour it down the sink and fill the bottle with water, hoping it's safe to drink.

"If you want people to leave you alone, just pretend you're drinking," Shauna told me one time, "and never ever leave your drink unattended."

I decide to go upstairs and check on Tara. I pick my way through the kids playing caps at the bottom of the stairs and standing around the kitchen. I don't see Tara anywhere, but I do come across Jodi.

"Hey, it's Mac!" she says, grabbing my hand. "Where you been, Mac?"

"Watching the skills competition."

She stumbles against me and apologizes. "Guess I'm a little wasted!"

"You look great, Jodi." Truth to tell, I am lying through my teeth. Her mascara is streaky, and her thick black hair, which was arranged in an updo at one time, is now tilted at a bizarre angle.

"You think so?" She looks at me with these big, brown eyes, then suddenly claps her hands and hollers, "Listen everybody! I wanna say something! Shut off the friggin' music!"

It takes a while for the message to get through to the person closest to the stereo. In the meantime, Jodi has climbed onto the island in the centre of her kitchen. She is very unsteady, so several hands reach out to help her stay aloft.

"I want to make a toast!" she shouts, holding up her drink.

"A toast! A toast!" the chant begins. Soon more people are squeezing into the kitchen.

I'm feeling foolish and also fearful for Jodi's safety.

"A toast to Mac!" Jodi announces. She looks down at me in dismay. "What's your real name again?" she asks in a loud stage whisper.

When she starts to lean towards me, she loses her balance and nearly plunges off the island, but hands grasp her and push her back to an upright position. She spills most of her drink on me. Great. Now I smell like a booze factory. How will I explain that to my parents?

"Jessie McIntyre!" I shout, afraid she will lean over again.

"Right, Jessie McIntyre," she slurs, raising what's left of her drink. "I want to propose a toast to Jessie McIntyre!"

"Damn right!" a male voice bellows.

"Jessie's one hell of a hockey player and my personal friend for two whole weeks!" She looks down at me and winks. "What some of you may not know is that Jessie has a...deep...dark...secret!" The timbre of her voice deepens dramatically with each of her last three words.

Now I'm afraid for myself. What's she going to say?

Jodi raises her arms and proclaims in the voice of an evangelist, "Jessie used to play...ringette!"

I sigh with relief.

"But soon after Jessie came to Estevan, she saw a vision! Now she too worships the gods of hockey at the great frozen cathedral! A toast! A toast to Jessie McIntyre!" She tosses the rest of her drink down her throat and steps trustingly off the table, falling straight into the waiting arms of four hockey players. They bear her like a high priestess, laughing and shrieking, out of the room.

The kitchen is filled with the clinking of bottles and shouted toasts, and the loud music resumes. I am now the centre of attention for several guys from Mark's team. One of them is Greg Kolenick, the goaltender. Correction — the starting goaltender.

"Nice to see you again, Jessie," Greg says. "Don't get out much, do you?"

"No, I don't." And I am definitely trying to do something about that.

"So how do you like Estevan?" another one asks.

I actually have to say very little. Any answer I give seems to please them immensely. Greg, as usual, is eager to brag himself up. He tells me all about a recent suspension for punching a Yorkton player with his blocker.

"Do you need another drink?" he asks after a while.

"No, I'm fine." I hold up my trusty bottle. "I just started this one."

He snatches it out of my hand. "Feels pretty warm," he says. "Let me get you another."

Before I can say a word, he's pulling a beer out of a box on the table and twisting off the cap.

"Thanks." I take the cold beer from his outstretched hand.

Greg throws an arm around my shoulders, and the other guys start to drift away. "Do you find it warm in here? Want to step outside for a while?" he asks.

I'm feeling very warm. I'm also eager to find a place to pour out the contents of my beer bottle. This seems the best opportunity since I am clearly not going to get rid of Greg any time soon.

"Follow me." He takes my hand and leads me towards the French doors.

Jodi's back deck is deserted, largely because most of it is piled with snow. Greg dusts off one of the steps and invites me to sit down next to him. When I do so, he slips an arm around me again, but because I can now easily pour my drink in the bushes next to the railing, I don't move away. I just hope he can't hear the glugging sound the beer makes as it leaves the bottle.

"So tell me all about you and Mark," he says after taking a drink of his own beer.

"What do you mean?"

"Mark says you wouldn't go out with him. How come?"

"Excuse me, but I don't think that's any of your business."

"Course it's my business," he says.

"And why's that?"

"Because we all think you're hot, and we don't know why Mark gets so mad whenever one of us mentions your name in the dressing room."

Although part of me is pleased, the other half is disgusted. I decide to move the conversation to a slightly higher plane. "Mark's going out with Kim anyway."

Greg pulls a package of cigarettes out of his pocket. "Want one?"

I shake my head.

Greg lights his cigarette and takes a puff before dropping the bombshell. "Jessie, the only reason why Mark lets Kim hang around him is because she puts out. Do you know what I'm talking about?"

I jump away from him as if stung. "She does not!"

"Oh, yes, she does," Greg says positively. "I know that for a fact."

He proceeds to give me a few more juicy tidbits I don't ask for. I cover my ears with my hands.

"Mark isn't like that!" I shout at him.

He beckons to me with one hand. "Jessie, come sit down."

It's too late. I've already tossed aside my beer and started running through the knee-deep snow behind Jodi's house in my stocking feet. Fortunately I'm still wearing my hoodie.

I ignore Greg's voice, which is calling for me to come back. It isn't that cold out, but my breath billows around me as I run. It's a beautiful night and I can see for miles in three directions. Out here it's not so hard to block out every ugly thing Greg said about Mark and Kim. But soon my feet are frozen, and I turn back towards the house, carefully avoiding the deck. Greg isn't on the step anymore, so I assume he's gone inside. I make my way around the house to the front yard and climb over the porch railing.

My plan is to sneak back inside through the front door and find Tara. I'll tell her that I want to go home, and if Nathan won't take me, I'll call my dad. I'm really hoping that Plan A will work because Plan B has its shortcomings. My dad will send me to a nunnery if he sees what goes on at hockey parties.

Just as my hand touches the doorknob, the door opens, startling me. Mark steps outside. Before he closes the door, I get a quick look at the sea of faces staring and smirking at me. Obviously Greg told everyone at the party about my midnight ramble through the snow.

"I was just coming to look for you! What're you doing running around out here?" Mark grabs me by the shoulders and gives me a little shake.

"Let me go!" I scream, pulling away. "You're a creep!"

"What?"

"You heard what I said! I never want to see you again!" I'm sobbing by now.

He pulls me into his arms and holds my head against his shoulder. I fight him at first, but it feels so good that I eventually just lean against him and cry my eyes out. The whole time he keeps stroking my hair and murmuring in my ear, telling me it's all right.

He smells wonderful.

I suddenly realize that both my feet are totally numb, and I pull away from him and look down.

"You're not wearing any shoes!" he says, amazed. He turns to open the front door, but I stop him. There are faces peering out every window.

"I'm not going in there!"

Before I can say another word, he picks me up and carries me to his truck, which is parked behind a bunch of vehicles at the end of the driveway. After we're inside, he starts the engine, then removes my frozen socks and rubs my bare feet between his hands. He pulls a blanket out from behind the seat and covers me with it.

"Tell me what's going on," he says.

I shake my head.

"You drive me nuts." He shakes his own head. "What am I going to do with you?"

"You don't have to do anything with me," I say bitterly. "You've got Kim."

He stops rubbing my feet for a minute. "What's that supposed to mean?"

It's out before I can stop myself. "Greg told me about you and her."

He looks at me blankly, then resumes the massage. "What did he say?"

I can't think of a way to put it delicately, so I stare out the windshield.

"Jessie, look at me," he says.

I slowly turn my head and meet his gaze. His features are etched in moonlight. God, he's beautiful.

"I just want to know why you're so mad at me all the time." He pushes my feet off his lap and begins to move towards me on the seat. "Tell me," he says gently.

I shake my head and turn away. He leans towards me, and I feel his lips brush my hair first, then my temple, my cheek, the corner of my mouth.

"Tell me," he whispers.

I am hypnotized by his nearness and the sound of his voice. I blurt out, "Why did your parents split up?"

That sure breaks the spell in a hurry.

"What?"

"I mean — they seem like really nice people. And they seem to care about you, so what happened?"

Mark just stares at me for a while. "They are nice people," he finally says. "I just don't understand why you —"

A loud rapping on the passenger side window nearly gives me a heart attack. I can't see out because of the frost on the pane, so I use the switch to lower the window.

It's Kim naturally.

"What're you doing in there?" she demands. Then she sees how close Mark is sitting to me. Again, that amazing range of emotions. "You little bitch!" she screeches. She grabs two handfuls of my hair and starts dragging me through the window while Mark holds onto my waist and tries to pull me back inside. It's not a great feeling, I can tell you.

"Let her go!" someone shouts.

I suddenly realize that Riley is standing out there too. He's trying to pry Kim's fingers open, but he's not having much luck.

I do the only thing I can think of. I grab Kim by the ears and kiss her right on the mouth. She releases me immediately and backs away from the truck, sputtering and wiping her lips. I don't care if I get called a lesbian for it. I just want to keep my hair.

Later when we're on the way home in Nathan's car, I think about how unfair I am being to Riley. How can I go out with him – feeling the way I do about Mark? When I tell him we shouldn't go out anymore, Riley just shrugs.

"It's okay," he says. "I'm kinda used to it."

chapter twenty

The following weekend we play the first installment of a two-game/total point series against the Southern Wildcats. The series winner will advance to the Female Bantam A Provincial Tournament, which will be held ten days later. We manage to lose this first, crucial game 3-2.

Our hearts are broken. Despite all our big plans, it looks like the Wildcat jinx is going to defeat us again. Steve assures us that we can beat them by two goals in the final contest.

At Sunday practice he explains how.

"Okay, gals." He pulls out the white marker board he uses for diagramming plays. "We've made a few changes. Everybody listening?"

We nod.

"I'm moving Jodi back to defence," Steve says.

"So we're going to have 5 D now?" Kim asks.

"No, I'm moving you up to left wing, Kim. We'll have

two centres — Tara and Kathy — and three sets of wingers."

I'm grateful to be sitting down. Doesn't Steve know anything about Kim? I look across at Tara, and she gives me this helpless expression.

"So you're saying that I'm no good at defence, right? Even though I've been playing defence all my life." Kim sounds really ticked.

"I'm saying that I want you to give this a try," says Steve. "It can't hurt to try, can it? It's for the team. We'll be stronger this way."

Kim doesn't say anything more, so I guess that's a step in the right direction. I'm amazed when she actually puts a solid effort into the offensive drills. She gives no outward sign of poutiness — if you don't count the fact that she won't talk to any of us.

I know she's still furious with me for what she thinks happened at Jodi's party, and I can't really blame her. Funny thing is, she must be too embarrassed to tell anybody because no one at EJH seems to know about it — except for Riley of course. And he's still talking to me.

As for Mark, I haven't heard or seen him since I left Jodi's party. Maybe it's better that way because I cringe every time I think about it. There he was — all set to kiss me — and I have to go and ask him that stupid question about his parents' divorce. I mean — where did that come from? I can't understand why I keep putting my foot in my mouth every time I talk to him. I should have done everybody a favour and just been born mute or something.

About halfway through practice, we start working on more complicated drills, and Mr. Kowalski makes up this combination of wingers: Larissa and Amber, Teneil and Randi, Kim and me.

Why did I ever let him think Kim and I are getting along?

"**Y**ou girls have got a mental block about the Wildcats," Dad tells me on the way to Carnduff for Game Two. "Just pretend that you're playing someone else."

"I wish we were playing someone else," I reply. "And I wish I wasn't playing on a line with Kim Scott."

As we suit up in the visitors' dressing room of the Carnduff arena, the atmosphere is tense. By the time our coaches begin their pre-game pep talk, I feel like throwing up.

"Man, you'd think somebody died in here," Steve says.

As we step onto the ice, my nerves are spiralling out of control. I wonder if the other girls feel the same way.

Because it's a provincial matchup, there's a little more fan-fare than usual. Some local kids hook up a CD player to the sound system and play some blood-pumping AC/DC tunes during our warm-up. Next an announcer introduces the members of both teams, and we sing "O Canada" before the game commences.

I'm relieved when Mr. Kowalski sends out Kathy, Teneil and Randi for the opening faceoff, even though it means I have to stand next to Kim on the bench. As soon as the referee drops the puck, Mr. Kowalski leans over my shoulder and whispers, "Stop worrying."

Despite the fact that we have three sets of wingers, Steve still wants short shifts. Kim and I step onto the ice before even a minute of play expires. Fortunately, Kathy dumps the puck deep into the Wildcats' zone before leaving the ice. Tara, Kim and I charge in and tie up their defence and centreman before they can break out.

Tara is working her magic behind the net while Kim and I try to stay open for a pass. The puck darts out to Kim, whose shot at the net goes wide. I drive into the corner after the puck and finally dig it out from between the Wildcat defenceman's skates. Seeing that Kim is down on her knees in front of the net, I push the puck over to Tara, who attempts a wraparound. The goalie gets there in time to stop her, but Kim flails at the puck and stuffs it in under her pads.

The red light goes on.

The goal isn't pretty, but I could care less.

"Start the bus for Rosetown, girls!" Kim screams.

· "I think Kim's going to like playing left wing," Tara says to me as we skate to the bench. "She likes getting points."

Although we manage to stay out of the penalty box in the first period, we fail to score on three power plays. I also notice that Kim only passes to me when absolutely necessary. Once she even banks the puck off the boards right into the path of three Wildcats, rather than give me a pass when I'm wide open. I bite my lip but smirk inwardly when Mr. Kowalski says something to Kim as we come off the ice. She just gives him a dirty look.

Then, with only fourteen seconds left on the clock, a brilliant pass from Jodi sends Kathy and Larissa into the Wildcat zone. At the opportune moment, Kathy puts the puck right on Larissa's tape, and Larissa launches the puck top left corner. They salute one another with the blades of their sticks and bow in acknowledgment of our wild cheers. The first period ends with us out in front 2-0.

The atmosphere in the dressing room is electric.

Mr. Kowalski proudly informs us that we outshot the Wildcats 11-7.

"Really?" says Miranda dryly. "I *thought* it seemed a little lonely at my end."

"That was smart to move Jodi back to defence, Coach," observes Shauna.

"And what about Kim on the wing?" Tara says quickly. "She's playing great!"

Steve nods, then points a big finger at me. "Mac, you just played your best period of hockey ever. Nice work in the corners."

"Gimme a break," Kim mutters under her breath. Neither of the coaches hears her.

The Wildcat squad that takes the ice in Period Two is determined to skate us into oblivion. It's all we can do to keep pace with their speedy first and second lines. By the end of the second period, the score is tied 2–2.

In the dressing room between periods, Mr. Kowalski reports that shots on goal are even at 23. I'm exhausted, and I don't need any statistical evidence to convince me that the tide is turning in favour of the opposition.

Vaguely, I hear Steve talking about not losing our focus, about hanging on for just twenty more minutes. Scoring two more goals in the third period seems impossible.

"This is a team sport, girls," Steve cautions. "Play as a team, skate hard, and we'll get the bounces. The Wildcats have a habit of resorting to one-man shows when the chips are down."

"Coach, have you ever seen the Wildcats when the chips are down?" asks Tara, sweat coating her upper lip. "I sure haven't."

As we head out for the third period, Tara reaches over the boards and murmurs something in her dad's ear. Steve starts in surprise, and a look of alarm spreads across his face as Tara skates to centre ice.

"What did she tell you?" I ask him.

Steve blushes and turns away. "Mac, mind your own business."

Tara wins the faceoff and drops the puck back to Carla, who retreats, finds open ice, and drives into the neutral zone. When a Wildcat winger challenges her, she passes to Amber, who shoots the puck deep into Wildcat territory. Tara chases it in, with Randi moving into the high slot. The Wildcat goaltender comes out of her net to play the puck and fans on the shot. Tara snaps the puck back to Randi, whose wrist shot ripples the twine in the back of the net. The referee points at the net, signalling the goal.

"We're up!" Mr. Kowalski shouts. "One more to go!"

We play the rest of the third period on pure adrenaline. Just like Steve predicted, the Wildcats quit playing as a team. Individual players make rushes and ignore passing opportunities.

"You can't win a hockey game all by yourself," observes Mr. Kowalski. "We just need to bide our time."

Yeah, but we're tiring, I think to myself. How can we possibly hang on to a one-goal lead, much less score another goal?

Things quickly go from bad to worse when Kathy takes a cross-checking penalty with seven minutes left in the game.

Then during the penalty kill, Kim receives a game misconduct after she checks one of the Wildcats' best players from behind. Even I have to admit the call was questionable. The Wildcat turned at the last minute, and Kim couldn't stop in time. Luckily, the girl had her head up when she went into the boards and wasn't hurt. We get a five-minute major because the ref says there was intent to injure. Steve questions him earnestly for a few minutes, then nods grimly and sends Amber to the box to serve the penalty. Kim leaves the ice without a word.

"I can't believe she's not putting up a fuss," says Teneil.

"We better not lose this game on account of those penalties," Mr. Kowalski mutters to himself as Tara and I step out of the box for the faceoff. "A five on three? And then three and a half minutes short-handed? What next?"

Darting a glance at Steve's dark face, I can almost feel sorry for Kim. Almost.

Our fans keep up a steady stream of cheering and foot stomping throughout the penalty. Somehow we manage to scrape through the next five minutes without allowing a Wildcat goal. I have never seen Larissa and Teneil play with more tenacity. Miranda makes miraculous saves to keep us in the game.

However, the kill takes its toll, and with a minute left to play, we're worn out. Steve calls a time out to give us a chance to suck down some air, then lightens the mood by telling this corny joke about a three-legged dog looking for the man who shot his paw.

"We don't have to score this period," he says when the referee's whistle ends the time out. "All you have to do is stop them from scoring. Then we can take a five-minute rest and get ready for overtime. Push them wide. We own the middle of the ice. Got it?"

We nod tiredly. We don't feel like we own anything.

Amber, who has the freshest legs because of her lengthy stopover in the penalty box, lines up with Tara and Teneil. Steve puts Shauna and Carla out on D.

The Wildcats' coach has sent out his best five players.

"Just let us get out of here alive," I breathe.

The linesman drops the puck.

I never knew that sixty seconds could seem so long.

Tara wins the faceoff and feathers a pass back to Carla, who eats up some time on the clock by cycling the puck along the boards to Shauna. A Wildcat winger forces Shauna to cough it up, but Tara poke-checks her doggedly. She nearly earns a slashing penalty when the ref half-heartedly raises his arm. The Wildcat fans howl in protest when he lowers it again. Shauna, who's trying to push a Wildcat out of the slot, deflects a shot. Miranda throws herself on the puck. The whistle blows.

Twenty-seven seconds left.

Steve sends out Kathy, Larissa and me. Jennifer and Jodi replace Carla and Shauna on D. I take a deep breath to quell the butterflies in my stomach and look over at Jodi, who winks.

The puck drops. Kathy is mowed over by the huge Wildcat centreman, who picks up the puck and charges the net. While I try to poke the puck away, Miranda hurtles out of her net and throws herself on top of it. I can scarcely believe my ears when the referee tells Miranda, with three Wildcats surrounding her, to play the puck. When Miranda refuses to yield, she gets a penalty for delay of game.

"That's a cheap call, ref!" someone shouts. It sounds like Dad.

With nineteen seconds left on the clock, I find myself in the box, serving Miranda's penalty. As the Wildcats line up once again in our zone, they look a little too self-assured.

"You're not going to score. We've worked too hard to get this far," I say out loud.

The next nineteen seconds drag. My four teammates valiantly try to keep the Wildcats from getting a decent shot on net, but Miranda is besieged by black rubber. I have never seen her play this well. With seconds left on the clock, Jodi gets possession of the puck and tries to ice it. A Wildcat defenceman redirects it with her stick and the puck rolls out past the blue line where Kathy snaps it up and explodes down the ice on a breakaway. With a Wildcat riding in her back pocket, she somehow manages to deke the goalie out of her shorts and slide the puck into the net on her stick side. It's the most beautiful goal of the season.

The Xtreme bench erupts, and every player swarms Kathy on the ice. As I go to join them, I see a lonely player standing on the other side of the glass, still wearing her uniform.

"I'm sorry, guys," Kim says after we are finally finished celebrating and shaking hands with a cowed Wildcat team. "I wish I could have been out there to celebrate. Did you see that cheap checking-from-behind penalty I got?"

Shauna stares solemnly at Kim. "Maybe you couldn't help it, but the ref had to make the call. You hit her square in the numbers."

"Only because she turned at the last minute!" Kim replies.

Steve puts his arm around Kim's neck and drags her towards the dressing room, murmuring in her ear. Kim pulls away from him as if stung and marches off to talk to her mother. Steve just stands there and stares after her. It isn't hard to tell what he's thinking.

"That girl needs an attitude adjustment." Tara unsnaps her chinstrap and yanks off her helmet. "Still, it's too bad she has to sit out the next game. We could really use her."

"We have another game this week?" I ask.

"Thursday night. We play the Peewee Boys' AA team. Dad thought we could use the game to help get ready for provincials."

I have a sudden thought. "You mean – he scheduled a game with the boys *before* we played the Wildcats? He's always telling us not to get cocky. He must have been pretty confident we would win."

Tara laughs. "Oh, he was confident all right. He told the guys at the Carnduff detachment that he'd shave his head if we lost the series to the Wildcats. I reminded him just before we started Period Three."

So that's what made him blush.

chapter
twenty-one

The trip to Rosetown has, in Mr. Kowalski's words, an inauspicious start.

First of all, the Bilkus are a half-hour late — but that should come as no surprise to anyone, since Larissa is nearly always the last one to arrive for practices and games.

Mrs. Bilku apologizes as she climbs onto the bus. "Larissa shouldn't have left her packing until the last minute, and then she couldn't find one of her elbow pads. I hope we haven't inconvenienced anyone."

The parents smile and nod, but I can tell they are annoyed.

Then Mr. Parker realizes that he forgot to pick up Kathy's skates from the local sporting goods store where he took them for sharpening.

"Now does everybody have everything?" Steve asks as a red-faced Mr. Parker climbs back aboard the bus, the nearly forgotten skates tucked underneath his arm. "It's nearly two o'clock, and it's a long drive." He surveys the sea of anxious faces. "If anyone needs to use the washroom, please use the one on the bus. We won't be waiting for anyone to use a public restroom if we have time to stop and grab a bite to eat."

I sit with Crystal, our backup goaltender, near the middle of the bus while my parents ride up front. The only parents missing on the trip are the Scotts. Kim's brother has a hockey tournament in Weyburn, so both her mom and dad are there for the weekend. I feel sorry for Kim, because it's obvious her parents don't respect girls' hockey. Still, I don't feel sorry enough to want either of the Scotts along. Mrs. Scott is always screaming at the officials and Mr. Scott's always screaming at us. Jodi's mom and dad aren't like that at all. It makes me wonder why parents act the way they do at hockey games. Do they come preprogrammed or do they learn bad behaviour from other parents?

My sister Courtney and Katelyn, Tara's little sister, are sitting a few rows up, watching a movie on a portable DVD player. Over the course of the season, they've become really tight – in spite of the four-year age gap. It's cool how our hockey team has helped our parents and siblings form friendships. It's like we're family.

All of a sudden I hear Kim's loud laugh, and I remember that our hockey family has some annoying relatives. She's playing poker at the back with Shauna, Carla and Kathy, and even though I'd love to go back there and socialize with the rest of the girls, I'm in no mood to deal with Kim.

"I'm glad that Randi and Jodi could come along, but Kim sure has a lot of opinions, doesn't she? At least her dad couldn't make it. He yells all the time," Crystal says, as she digs her iPod out of her knapsack. "Anyway, we're gonna do awesome in this tournament. I hope I get to play at least one game."

"I'm going to go sit over there." I gesture to some empty seats across the aisle. "I want to take a nap."

"Sure," Crystal says. "Good idea."

I settle myself in my new location, then put on my sunglasses and headphones and try to fall asleep, listening to my MP3 player. I didn't get much sleep last night, so eventually I doze off. I wake up when Kathy plops down beside me.

"Where are we?" I ask groggily.

"About halfway," Kathy responds. "Want to play some cards? We're just starting a new game, and there's an empty seat next to Kim."

I shake my head. "No thanks."

Kathy furrows her brow. "Hey, you're not being very sociable. Is something wrong?"

I am grateful for my sunglasses, which hide the tears that have sprung to my eyes. My emotions seem very close to the surface lately.

"Just nervous." I try to sound casual.

"Well, I'm feeling the same way myself – with your dad on the same bus. I can't even concentrate on that poker game."

"Right." I turn my head towards the window and watch the prairie scenery fly by.

"Just relax. And remember – this road trip is the perfect finish for our season. Try to enjoy it." Kathy stands up and moves to the back of the bus.

Now I know why I'm feeling down. I've loved everything about playing hockey this year – even with Kim on the team. It's all going to be over by Monday, and eight months will go by before I get to play again.

Even worse, will I stay in touch with the girls during the off-season? Will they all be back to play midget girls' hockey next year?

By then they might not even remember my name.

Our bus rolls into Rosetown at 7:30 that evening. We scarcely have enough time to drop off our bags at our motel, grab our jerseys and board the bus to head for the rink.

During the opening ceremonies, the participating teams skate or walk into the arena, each one led by two minor hockey players wearing Rosetown sweaters and holding a

sign bearing the team's name. There are six teams — us,
Regina, Saskatoon, Prince Albert, Swift Current and
Rosetown, the host team. A girl who looks no older than we
do plays the bagpipes. Two or three local dignitaries, as well as
representatives from the Saskatchewan Hockey Association,
welcome us. During the speeches, I examine the numerous
banners hanging from the roof of the arena. Apparently
Rosetown teams — both young and old — have been very suc-
cessful in league and provincial competition. Despite the fact
that my knees are trembling, I'm bursting with pride just to
be here. When I come off the ice, my parents and Courtney
are there to greet me. Mom's eyes are shiny with tears.

Back at the motel, we go to Steve's room for a team
meeting. He reminds us that our first pool game against
Saskatoon will be played the following morning at eight. We
will then play Rosetown at 3:30. I wonder briefly if I will
know anybody on the Saskatoon team.

"We don't have to finish first in our pool," Mr. Kowalski
explains. "It's the same format as the Regina tournament."

"That means four games in two days." Steve looks deadly
serious. "Make sure you get your beauty sleep. There'll be no
time for tossing chairs in the pool tonight."

Kathy blushes. "Right you are, Coach."

Steve continues. "We meet for breakfast at 6:30 tomorrow
in the dining room. No ordering off the menu. The motel

staff is preparing a continental breakfast according to my instructions."

"No Belgian waffles?" Miranda asks.

"Absolutely not — at least not until after the game. Oh, and girls, we have a special surprise for you."

Mrs. Brewer pulls a large box out from behind one of the double beds. She opens the flaps on the box and removes a black windbreaker with the Xtreme logo sewn on the front.

Very cool.

"Shauna, this is yours." She points to the number four on the sleeve.

"That's nice that Shauna gets a new jacket," Crystal says politely. "My mom says she's a really good captain."

Everyone groans.

"Crystal, think about it," Kathy says. "We all get jackets!"

Mrs. Brewer quickly finds herself surrounded by players, waiting impatiently for theirs. As I pull mine on, I admire the way my name is stitched on the left sleeve with a number thirteen on the right.

"Who bought these anyway?" Carla asks. "Do we have a team sponsor?"

"You have a whole bunch of sponsors," Mrs. Brewer replies. "They're called your parents. Don't forget to thank them."

"Can I just wear my Bantam A jacket?" Kim asks. "It's black."

All the girls gawk at her. Tara's mom looks hurt.

Steve stares at Kim for a long moment. "You wear the jacket of the team you're playing for." He pauses, then addresses all of us. "Okay, meeting's over. Lights out in ten minutes. Dress code in effect all day tomorrow. If we look like a team, we'll play like a team."

The following morning in the dressing room, Mrs. Brewer hands each of us a small pin representing the Energy City.

"What are we supposed to do with these?" asks Amber. "I think I already have one at home."

"You give them to the opposition." Kim shakes her head scornfully.

"It's a goodwill gesture," explains Mrs. Brewer. "If you're lucky, the Saskatoon players might give you pins too."

"I doubt that very much," Miranda says. "Not after what they said to us at the motel last night."

Kathy grins from ear to ear. "We've already been doing some PR."

Tara's mom looks concerned. "I don't think I want to hear this."

"The Saskatoon girls said our team was from the sticks and didn't stand a chance," Larissa blurts out, "but that was after Kathy told them we're going to kick their asses."

That's when Shauna says, "Parker, maybe you better avoid players from the other teams or learn to shut your mouth. Acting first and thinking later isn't going to cut it here."

I can't believe my ears. In the three and a half months I've been playing with the Xtreme, I've never heard Shauna speak that way to one of her teammates.

Kathy sits down on the bench and sullenly reties one of her skates.

Awkward silence.

Tara's the first to break it. "Thanks for getting the pins, Mom," she says.

"I think everyone has pre-provincial jitters," Mrs. Brewer says. "Once you're on the ice, you'll be okay."

During the warm-up, I look in the stands for my family and find them sitting near centre ice with the rest of the Xtreme fans. At the other end of the rink, a full squad of eighteen Saskatoon skaters takes turns warming up both goaltenders. I don't recognize any of the players.

Miranda starts in net, and Crystal seems content with her role of running the door for the defence.

We play Steve's system for the first two periods and move out in front 5-1. Things start falling apart early in the third, however, when some of us quit skating and let Saskatoon beat us to the puck.

None of Steve or Mr. Kowalski's warnings do any good, and after five minutes, the tide starts turning. The Saskatoon team begins to capitalize on our mistakes and gradually chips away at our lead until they trail by only two goals. They gain momentum with every shift, just like a snowball rolling down a hill. For the first time all year, we start sniping at one another, blaming linemates for our own shortcomings.

It's ugly hockey — the worst.

With less than two minutes left on the clock, Saskatoon scores yet another goal, and Steve quickly calls a time out.

"Look, ladies," he waves a finger in each of our faces, "if some of you think that a tie's not so bad, then I'm here to tell you we definitely *don't* want to take that route."

"The last time I looked at the scoreboard, we were still winning," Kim says.

"Yes, we're still winning." Steve makes a visible effort to control his temper. "But you won't be if you keep playing this bush league hockey. Is this what you came here to do?"

We shake our heads.

"Listen," says Steve, "I was talking to the coach from Regina this morning. He remembers you girls from the December tournament. He said you play great positional hockey — the best he's seen in a long time."

"He obviously wasn't including boys' hockey," Kim mutters.

"Oh, enough about boys' hockey already!" says Kathy.

Tara tries pumping us up as we skate onto the ice to faceoff deep in our own end. "Move your feet, girls! And play smart hockey, like Steve taught us."

"I'm getting tired of everyone talking about your dad like he's the great guru of hockey," says Kim. "He could learn a few things from my dad."

If Kim only knew how much we love Mr. Scott.

We manage to hang on to our one-goal lead, but there's no celebration in the dressing room after the game. Instead Kathy and Tara keep exchanging insults with Kim. It's a bad time for them to decide they've had enough of her smart remarks.

"You're just jealous because I got more goals in that game than you did," Kim says at one point.

Kathy swears under her breath and storms out of the dressing room.

To make matters worse, Teneil and Miranda talk incessantly about going to Saskatoon to watch the Midget Bruins play, even though everyone insists there's no time to get there and back before 3:30.

"And how are you going to get to Saskatoon anyway?" Kim demands. "Do you think the great guru of hockey is going to let you take his precious bus?"

"Will you quit calling him that?" Tara retorts.

By now the two of them are standing jaw to jaw. I look at Shauna, hoping she'll do something. But she isn't even looking at them. She just goes on unlacing her skate as if nothing's wrong. What's wrong with her? Can't she see what's happening to us?

Carla finally puts a stop to it by stepping between Kim and Tara.

"Cool down, girls," she says. "Let's focus on Game Two, okay?"

I'm relieved when all three of them sit down again. Nobody says much after that.

I dread the next game.

chapter twenty-two

ilence reigns in the dressing room when we return to the arena for Game Two against the Rosetown Rockets. I don't know which is worse – the catty remarks or the unwholesome quiet.

Both coaches seem unaware of the decline in team morale. Instead of keeping us focused and grounded, Steve and Mr. Kowalski always seem to be watching the other teams and sizing up the competition.

Mrs. Brewer finally comes in to tell us that Regina has beaten Swift Current 4-2.

"That's good news," observes Miranda. "Maybe Regina isn't that strong after all."

"It means nothing." Shauna takes a roll of white tape out of her bag. "We don't know anything about Swift Current."

"If we played more teams from around the province – like the boys do – then we'd know how good the competition is," Kim declares.

Tara stands up and ties the lace that holds up her pants. "Kim, why are you here if you think girls' hockey is so crappy?"

Kim is immediately on the defensive. "I never said girls' hockey was crappy! I might say it's inferior, but I'd never say it's crappy!"

"Somebody shut her up, before I hit her," Kathy mutters.

I look hopefully in Carla's direction, but she just keeps on taping her stick.

"Girls! Girls!" Mrs. Brewer holds up her hands. "You won't have a sniff at beating Rosetown if you keep fighting amongst yourselves. Honestly, I don't know what's wrong with the lot of you." She pauses to do a quick survey of our state of dress. "I'm going to get Steve. Try not to kill one another before I get back."

Kim reopens the debate as soon as Mrs. Brewer is gone. "You girls are just jealous because Jodi and I play for elite teams."

"Leave me out of this," Jodi says.

I can tell that Tara is fuming. "Kim, when was the last time you played a regular shift with the Bantam As? October?"

"You shut your mouth! You don't know *anything* about me and the Bantam A team!" Kim screams, advancing on Tara.

Tara just stands there, waiting for her.

No one breathes.

Amber's voice is shaking when she speaks. "If all we're going to do is fight amongst ourselves, then we might as well have stayed home. We need to start acting like a team."

"You call this a team?" Kim forgets about Tara and glares at Amber. "You're even more stupid than I thought!"

Amber's face goes pure white while Kathy's turns red. She stands up.

Oh, oh. Hurry up, Steve.

"Quit picking on Amber!" Kathy says. "She's never done anything to you! Why don't you pack up your gear and go home?"

Carla whistles appreciatively. "Thank you, Kathy!"

"You can't be talking to me." Kim smiles smugly. "Who's going to score all your points if I leave?"

"Will someone please stuff a sock in her mouth?" Kathy says. "I can't stand it anymore!"

"I'll stuff a sock in *your* mouth!" Kim cries, turning on Kathy.

That's when I realize that we need to sort this out for ourselves. Until I make things right with Kim, we are never going to be a team again. It's just like that thing with Marsha. If you don't confront a bully — and get someone else to help you do it — they're never going to go away.

I stand up.

"Kim, we're all trying hard to make a place for you on this team, but you're not making it easy. We don't want you to leave, but we're not putting up with your attitude anymore. Would it be so hard for you to admit you like playing with us?"

I make the mistake of placing a hand on Kim's shoulder.

She whirls around and slaps me right across the face. "Don't touch me!"

I stagger under the force of the blow. My lip is bleeding.

Carla and Shauna jump up and grab hold of Kim before she can hit me again. Kim swears at both of them and struggles to free herself. She's so angry, I barely recognize her anymore. Her eyes are bulging out of her head.

"This is all your fault!" she shrieks. "No matter how well I play, Tara's dad likes you better! And so does Mark! It's not fair! I've wanted Mark for years – and then you come along and spoil everything! Everything!"

Here we go with the dirty laundry in the dressing room again. I am totally bowled over. The stuff about Mark comes as no surprise, but I had no idea Kim even cared what Steve thought of her.

"Kim, I've never done anything to make Mark think I like him."

"I can testify to that," says Tara.

By now Kim is drawing ragged breaths and sobbing. It's painful to watch. "It's always 'Jessie, way to cover your man' and 'Way to take away the passing lanes'! All he ever says to me is, 'No use going in the corner and then passing to where you're supposed to be'!"

I gather she's talking about Steve, not Mark. "Steve tries to say nice stuff to you, but every time he does, you make some crack about boys' hockey. Can't you just say 'thanks' once in a while?"

"Jessie's right, Kim," says Shauna. "You should listen to her."

Kim keeps struggling, but she's getting tired, I can tell. "I'm not listening to any of you! You're all snotty bitches — every one of you!"

"Kim, take a pill already," Jodi says. "We didn't come all this way to watch you make a fool of yourself."

"You just shut right up!" Kim shouts. "I'm sick of hearing about the great Jodi Palmer! You're not nearly as good as you think you are!"

Jodi shakes her head and sighs. "Whatever."

I choose my next words very carefully. "And that's another thing. You've got to quit comparing yourself to Jodi. Sure she's a great player, but it takes all kinds of players to make a team. Maybe you're not as good as her, but you *are* good. We all know it, don't we, girls?"

I pause for a second to let the rest of the girls chime in, which they do wholeheartedly.

"You have to quit blaming everyone else when things go wrong. Sometimes life just sucks — and it's nobody else's fault."

"Whoa," says Kathy.

"That should be on a poster or something," says Teneil.

Kim just stands there, her chest heaving. Shauna and Carla are still clutching her arms, but it's more like they're holding her up — not holding her back.

"What are you talking about?" Kim says. "That doesn't make any sense!"

"It sure does," says Jodi. "It was tough breaking my collarbone in the middle of my best season, but —"

"Shut up!" says Teneil. "You're gonna make it worse! Just let Jessie talk!"

Thirteen faces pivot towards me, waiting expectantly for my next words of wisdom.

But I've run dry. I can't think of anything else to say. "That's it." I shrug helplessly.

"Will you let me go please?" Kim asks. "I want to take off my equipment."

The two girls release her. She immediately sits down on the bench and starts unlacing her skates. Everyone watches her in anxious silence.

I don't want to say it — at least part of me doesn't — but I know it's up to me. "Kim, if you leave, you'll have no place to play. We're your team, and we need you. You know you belong with us."

Kim shakes her head.

"You could just apologize," Tara says. "It's easier than leaving."

Kim pulls off one skate and angrily slams it into her hockey bag. "I am not apologizing."

From where I'm sitting, I can see that a huge droplet is forming beneath her nose. It splashes on the black mat beneath her feet when she bends over to remove her other skate.

Tara implores, "Just say you're sorry, Kim. We want you to play with us — but Jessie's right. Your attitude sucks, and it's got to change."

Kim's other skate lace has resolved itself into a hard knot. She yanks at it, but it won't come loose.

"Come on. Apologize. We'll forgive you," says Kathy.

The hands wrestling with the knot stop moving. They tense into fists, then relax.

"Okay." Kim sighs and straightens up. "I'm sorry for what I said about girls' hockey — and Tara's dad. I didn't mean it."

We breathe a collective sigh of relief.

"And I'm sorry I called you stupid, Amber." Her voice actually sounds sincere. "And Jodi — any team would be lucky to have a player like you. Anything else?"

"Make your peace with Jessie once and for all," says Shauna.

Kim shakes her head. "No way."

"Do it," says Tara. "As Dad would say, bury the hatchet."

"A dangerous suggestion, if I ever heard one," says Carla.

We all turn our heads at the sound of running footsteps and a fist hammering on the door.

"Speak of the devil," says Kathy.

"You better all be decent!" Steve shouts. "Because we're coming in!"

A distraught Steve, Mr. Kowalski and Mrs. Brewer explode into the dressing room.

"What's this I hear about a fight? Is everyone okay?" Steve's eyes drill two holes through Tara.

"Everything's fine." I cover my cut lip with my fingers. "We're ready to play."

"Well, almost all of us," Kim says, blushing. "Is anybody good with knots?"

As most of the girls leave the dressing room, Shauna gestures for me to stay behind.

"Thanks for stepping in," she says. "I could never have done what you did."

I'm amazed. "You and Carla stopped her from hitting me!"

Shauna shakes her head. "I was angry after the Saskatoon game. We played terrible, and for a while, I *did* wish I was back playing boys' hockey."

I nod.

"I sure hope you're gonna play midget girls' next year." Shauna grins and adds, "And what about this summer? Do you play softball?"

Suddenly next season doesn't feel so far away.

We play the game of our lives against Rosetown. After allowing a couple of weak goals, Miranda settles down to business. Thanks to Tara, Kathy, Jodi and Amber, we rally back from a three-goal deficit and move ahead 4-3 by the final buzzer. Best of all, we're having fun again. Everyone's laughing and talking to one another on the bench and in the dressing room – well, almost everyone.

Kim doesn't say a word to me, but she passes the puck when I'm open. I can live with that.

"We've won our pool, girls!" Steve tells us in the dressing room afterward. "Tomorrow we'll play either Regina or Prince Albert. It depends on who loses tonight."

That night after supper, we go back to the arena and watch Regina beat Prince Albert 7-6 in overtime.

"This is good hockey," Crystal says to me on the bus on our way back to the motel. "All the games have been close."

The Xtreme gather in Shauna's room to unwind.

"Dad says Prince Albert has a weak third line." Amber stretches out on the carpet and groans. "I sure hope I get to play against them because every muscle in my body is sore."

"Just one more game between us and the A final," says Crystal. "I can't believe it."

"Tomorrow we better be wearing our game faces," says Shauna. "And if we make it past PA, we better be ready for Regina. I bet they walk all over Rosetown in the semi, and they'll be gunning for us, seeing as how we embarrassed some of them in the Regina tournament."

Kathy tosses a pillow at my head. "I'll bet Number 11 will have her eyes open when you're on the ice!" she crows. "Remember how you decked her for blindsiding Larissa?"

"I haven't forgotten," Larissa says. "You're still my knight in shining armour, Jessie."

I stifle a yawn, then stand up and stretch. "Well, this knight is going to get some shut-eye. See you tomorrow."

As I pass the Howards' room, I hear the sound of adult laughter. I stop and listen for a minute. My dad's telling the story of how I got started in hockey. He's so excited about this tournament, you'd think he was playing.

"Hey, Jessie. Wait up a sec."

I turn around. Kim is shuffling down the hallway towards me, wearing a big pair of cow slippers.

What now?

"I wanted to give you something," Kim says when she reaches me. She looks very uncomfortable, like she'd rather be someplace else. She holds out her hand and opens it, revealing a large metal disc.

I recognize it immediately. "Hey, that's my medal from the Regina tournament! Where'd you find it?"

"I didn't find it." Kim blushes. "I took it."

"T-took it?" I stammer. "When? How?"

"Never mind." Kim looks down at her slippers. "And I'm the one who sicced Marsha on you by spreading rumours on MSN."

"You think I don't know that?"

Kim looks at me, startled. "Man, you must really hate me." She continues. "Remember your bike? You thought that Marsha wrecked your tire – but she didn't. I did. And at the school dance, I wanted you to drink that rum and Coke – so I could get you suspended."

"Why are you telling me all this?"

"I don't really know." Kim looks at her feet again. "I guess I'm trying to say I'm sorry."

"What about Mark?"

She shrugs. "He broke up with me after Jodi's party – or I broke up with him. I'm not sure which. It's over, anyway."

"So what happens if he wants to go out with me?"

She rubs her finger under her nose and wipes it on her pajama pants. "Oh, he wants to go out with you, that's for sure. He's always liked you. I hate it, but I can't do anything about it." She sighs. "Look, I'm tired of being angry with you. I know we won't ever be friends — not after all the things we've said and done. But maybe we can stop being enemies."

I stare at the top of her head. Since I can't see her eyes, I don't know how sincere she is. Oh well, it's worth the risk.

"Sure."

Kim looks up and smiles. It looks as real as smiles come.

That night I have the best sleep I've had in a long time.

chapter
twenty-three

n Sunday we arrive at the rink around noon, then quickly dress and watch a little of the semifinal between Rosetown and Regina. The Rosetown team has overwhelming fan support. The third period is just starting when I squeeze between Shauna and Teneil, who are peering through the glass behind Regina's net.

"What's the score?" I ask.

"It's tied 2-2." Shauna points to the scoreboard. "But the Rockets just got the power play."

"Did anyone hear who won the consolation game?"

"Yeah, it was Swift Current — three minutes into over-time. The final score was 3-2," Kim says.

I watch the two teams battle it out for a few minutes. The Regina girls look very fast and skilled. I wonder how we will fare against them. We'll have to get past Prince Albert to find out.

"I've seen enough." Jodi turns her back on the glass. "I'm heading for the dressing room."

By the time we take the ice at one o'clock, Regina has earned a berth in the provincial final, beating Rosetown 5-2.

My parents are sitting in their usual place at centre ice. Our fans are never hard to find because Mrs. Howard made little black and gold pennants with the players' numbers on them. And my dad's wearing his Boston Bruins jersey. Courtney waves at me, and I wave back.

After the warm-up and the exchange of pins, Steve sends out Kathy, Kim, Jennifer, Jodi and me to take the opening faceoff against the Prince Albert Pikes. Proud of Steve's confidence in me, I take my place at centre ice and look over at Kim, who grins back.

The puck falls, and the semifinal is underway.

The Prince Albert coach does his best to match lines, but since we are the home team, we have the right of last change. Our best players are all over theirs, tying up their offence. Kathy sets up Randi and Carla with one goal apiece, then scores herself on a breakaway late in the period. By the end of the first period, the score is 3-0 for us, but the game is starting to get rough.

"If that Number 27 doesn't quit slashing me, I'm going to deck her." Kathy is seething. She pulls back her sleeve to show us the red welts on her forearms. "Is the ref blind?"

In Period Two, Kathy forces Number 27 to take a holding penalty. It backfires, however, because PA scores short-handed.

The rest of the period is marred by a number of penalties called on both teams. It's hard to find a rhythm with the whistle blowing so often.

"Why doesn't he just let us play?" Kathy whines. "Did he just buy a new whistle or what?"

"Before you were complaining because he didn't call enough." I poke her playfully in the ribs. "Make up your mind."

PA scores three more unanswered goals in the second period.

We now trail by one.

In the dressing room after Period Two, Kathy says, "I'd feel better if I could lower the boom on 27, but if I take another penalty, Coach'll kill me."

"Sounds like you're turning over a new leaf," Tara says.

Kathy shrugs. "Trying to." She looks over at Kim. "I notice you're being a good girl too. You must've learned a lesson when you had to sit out that game against the Peewee AAs."

Horrified, I try to make eye contact with Kathy. Isn't it a little early to start razzing Kim? What if she makes some nasty remark and upsets the whole team again?

"You girls should've worn orange jerseys for that game." Kim squirts some water in her mouth.

Oh-oh.

"Why's that?" Kathy's voice definitely has an edge.

Kim spits the water into the garbage can and wipes her lips before answering. "The way those guys skated around you, you looked like pylons."

It's dead quiet. Everyone's face has turned to stone.

Then Kim laughs — and for some reason, it doesn't sound annoying. "Good thing I wasn't out there. I would've been the biggest pylon of them all." She pauses for effect and adds, "You guys only have to put up with my dad once in a while. I have to *live* with him."

Thank goodness. I didn't mean it when I said it earlier, but maybe Kim actually does belong on this team.

Carla stands up and stretches the muscles in her lower back. "I'll tell you one thing." She winks at Kim and bares her teeth. " I'd sure like to live with your dad."

That sparks a chorus of yipping and howling. Kim blushes and sits down, but it looks like she's enjoying the attention.

And the team has finally found a new target for "hot dad." Life just doesn't get any better.

Two minutes into Period Three, Steve puts Kathy and Jodi out at the same time, with Tara centering the line and Shauna and Carla on defence.

If anybody can score, they can, I think to myself.

Kim points to the Wolves' coach, who is busily giving instructions to one of his players on the bench. "Steve must have caught him napping. He's still got his third line out there!"

Steve's strategy pays off as Tara wins the faceoff back to Shauna, and the Xtreme captain banks a perfect pass along the boards to Jodi. Jodi burns Number 27 and goes wide around Prince Albert's weakest defenceman. Her back-pass falls smack onto Tara's blade, and before the Wolves' netminder can react, the puck is in the net.

We're all tied up, and so the score remains until the buzzer sounds to end three periods of play.

Overtime.

After a few words from Steve and Mr. Kowalski, we file out of the dressing room for sudden death. A number of Regina players are loitering in the hallway, fully dressed apart from their helmets.

"Hey, score a goal, will ya?" one of them shouts. "We wanna polish the ice with you in the final!"

"Hey, Regina, you suck!" Kathy yells.

I hear someone calling my name just as I'm about to step on the ice. I look up into the stands and see Maggie Taylor standing next to my parents. She's waving at me and pointing at a tall, familiar figure beside her.

Mark.

My heart leaps into my throat. "What are you doing here?" I shout.

"I'll tell you later!" Mark shouts back. "Win the game!"

The rest of the Xtreme surge around me, trying to get to the gate.

"Quit blowing kisses!" Tara quips, giving me a playful shove. "Overtime waits for no one!"

Stunned, I skate to the players' box and sit down, knees trembling.

Kim stands over me. "I see you've brought some more fans," she says.

I blush and stammer. "I don't know why he's here."

"Right," she says, then points into the stands. "And how's a girl supposed to focus on the game with your dad wearing that sexy Boston Bruins jersey?"

I knew it was too good to last.

The puck drops to begin overtime, and I forget about Kim – and Mark – instantly. It takes every ounce of concentration to play my position and keep myself open for a pass.

By the ten-minute mark, it's clear that we're tiring. When twenty minutes of sudden death elapses, the winner is still undetermined.

"You girls are wearing yourselves out trying to put this game away," Steve tells us in the dressing room. "Be patient."

It's around this time that I begin wondering how we can

put up a fight against Regina – even if we do manage to beat Prince Albert. We have just played four periods of hockey, and every one of us is bushed. We don't have enough gas left to be provincial champs.

Three minutes into the second overtime, Prince Albert penetrates deep into our zone. Worn out, we are unable to clear the puck, and Miranda's extraordinary play is the only thing that keeps us in the game. Shauna lies down to block a shot, and I see the puck bounce back to PA's point man, the player I am supposed to be covering. I try to get back to tie her up, but she one-times a slapshot that rockets through the tangle of players screening Miranda and whizzes over her right shoulder. The twine behind her ripples as the puck bounces against it.

The goal judge's red light glows. The referee blows his whistle and points at the net.

Our provincial run is over.

In disgust, Miranda digs the puck out of the net and sends it flying. While the Prince Albert team piles on one another screaming, we stare in exhaustion and disbelief. We have just lost the last game of the season.

I throw down my stick in a gesture of self-loathing and start to skate away. I distantly hear someone calling my name, and then feel a hand grab my shoulder and pull me back. Turning, I can scarcely recognize Shauna through my tears.

"It's okay!" she's saying. "It's not your fault!"

"It *is* my fault! I hate myself!" I rip off my helmet and throw it on the ice.

Shauna picks up my helmet and hands it to me. "Let's show some class," she says.

As we gather around Miranda, every one of our faces is streaked with tears and sweat.

"We did our best," she says in a hoarse voice. "Shake hands with Prince Albert."

As we congratulate the other team, I force myself to look into their beaming faces. That should be us, I think resentfully. We deserve to be playing in the final.

Steve says the same thing in the dressing room later on. I have never seen him show so much emotion.

"I couldn't be prouder of you girls." His voice breaks. "You played hard right to the end. You'll always be champions in my book."

"Thanks, Coach." Carla echoes the sentiments of every player. "But it still hurts."

"I'll tell you what hurts," says Jodi after Steve and Mr. Kowalski leave. "What hurts is watching all you girls stand on your bottom lip. People, show a little levity. We'll win provincials next year."

"Does that mean you're gonna play midget girls'?" asks Kathy.

"Yeah, I'll be back," Jodi says, stretching. "This is way more fun than guys' hockey, isn't it, Bisonhead?"

Carla nods. "Yeah, all the guys do in the dressing room is swear and fart and squirt each other with their water bottles."

"Besides," Jodi says, looking at Kim, "if a girl wants to get noticed by university scouts, she better start playing the girls' game."

"Were there university scouts here?" Kim asks, flabbergasted.

Jodi nods. "You better believe it. My dad saw a guy wearing a University of Alberta jacket. And," she adds in a significant tone, "he had a zip-up binder."

"Wish my dad had been here to see that," Kim says.

"What about you, Kim? Are you gonna play midget girls' next year?" Kathy asks.

Everyone looks at Kim, waiting. Has her attitude really changed — or will she just make another crack about boys' hockey?

"I probably will," Kim says. "I kinda like playing with you pylons."

By the time everyone has showered, the atmosphere is considerably lighter. After I pack up my equipment, I emerge from the dressing room in a better mood. More than anything, I want to talk to Mark. A few of the girls are lined up along the glass, watching the provincial final, which has been underway for seven minutes.

"What's the score?" I ask.

Shauna replies, "3-0 for Regina."

"They should kiss our skates for taking PA into two over-time periods," says Jodi.

"Did you hear about Swift Current?" Tara smiles. "They want to form a midget girls' league with us next year. Dad thinks we can talk the Wildcats and Weyburn into joining. And he's going to work on the Notre Dame B team and Moose Jaw."

"A real league? That's awesome!" exclaims Kathy, pounding on the Plexiglas.

In the lobby, my family immediately surrounds me.

"You played a great game," Mom murmurs as she gives me a warm hug.

"I'm sorry we didn't make it to the final."

Dad squeezes my hand reassuringly. "It doesn't matter. We wouldn't have missed this for the world."

Courtney pulls on my sleeve. "Did you hear me and Katelyn cheering, Jessie?"

"Yes, I did." I give her a big hug. "You're our number one fans."

Out of the blue, Mom says, "Mrs. Taylor was telling us

about some situation you're involved in with a girl from the Comp. What's that about?"

I catch a glimpse of Mark in the crowd. This is no time for rehashing ancient history with my parents. "It's okay, Mom. She just had me mixed up with someone else."

"Who had you mixed up? That girl – or Mrs. Taylor?"

"Look, it's over. Everything's good now. I promise."

Mom and Dad look very concerned, and I can tell we're going to have a long talk when we get home. Hopefully I'll be able to get out of the house again before spring thaw.

Good thing Mrs. Brewer comes over and starts talking to my parents. I look for Mark, and he isn't far away.

"Tough game." He places a hand lightly on my shoulder. "You played well."

"Thanks." A thought occurs to me. "Why aren't you in Saskatoon?"

"Five of the guys decided to bring some booze along and get knee-walking drunk last night. Coach pulled us out of the tournament and sent us home."

"Wow. Why didn't he just bench the five guilty ones – instead of punishing the whole team?"

"Two of them were our goalies."

"Oh." It takes me a minute to put two and two together. "So one of them was Greg Kolenick."

"That's right," Mark looks at me intently. "And speaking of Kolenick, I'd like to know what he said to you at Jodi's party."

I raise my chin defiantly. "He told me some stuff about you and Kim that wasn't very nice." Blushing, I give him a few of the details.

Mark stands there shaking his head in disbelief. "The guy's a loser, Jessie. He was probably just trying to get into your pants."

I don't really have a rejoinder for that one.

He takes a deep breath. "Look, I didn't really want to go out with Kim in the first place, but she just wouldn't go away. I kind of felt sorry for her – seeing how hard her parents push her all the time."

"I understand."

"I didn't even see much of her this winter – not with my hockey schedule and studying for SATs."

This confuses me. "I thought Tara said you want to go to university out East?"

"I don't want to close any doors, Jessie. I wouldn't turn down a good scholarship from an American university if it came along."

"I guess there's a lot about you I don't know." I pause for a moment. "I'm sorry for asking about your parents' divorce. That was really dumb."

"No, it wasn't. I'm glad you liked them." He takes my hand in his. "Jessie, Kim and I are finished. You're the one I've been thinking about all winter."

My heart is hammering in my ears. "Really?"

"Really. But if you're still going out with Riley —"

"I'm not! I broke up with him the night of Jodi's party."

"Wish I'd known that a few weeks ago," he says. "Sounds like we have lots to catch up on."

"I hate to interrupt." Mom taps me on the shoulder. "Jessie, you better get your stuff outside. Steve says the bus is leaving in five minutes."

"Okay, Mom."

"He also said you'll be stopping for supper on the way back." Mom hands me a twenty-dollar bill and gives me a hug. "Have a nice trip, honey."

Confused, I watch Mom walk away. "Why did she say goodbye to me just now?" I reach down to pick up my hockey bag.

Mark puts a hand on my forearm and gently pulls me back up. "I didn't make my mom drive like a bat out of hell all the way from Saskatoon so I could watch you carry your equipment." He throws the bag onto his broad shoulder. "Which way to the bus?"

"It's out back," I explain, hurrying to keep up with his long strides. "Too bad you can't come with us."

"And who says I can't?" He stops and turns halfway round. "Your family's riding home with my mom. We got all friendly during your game." He pauses to let the news sink in. "Guess I'll finally get to see what a girls' hockey team does on a road trip. Any chance one of you will give me a make-over?" He winks.

As I follow him out of the rink, I think to myself — maybe there won't be a Female Bantam A Provincial Championship banner hanging in the Civic this year. But there's sure as hell going to be a midget banner next year.

And I'll be there to watch it go up.

author's note

I firmly believe that bullying has *always* been with us. It's not a bizarre aberration of the 20th or 21st centuries. However, thanks to mass media, we are now more aware of bullying. The Reena Virk case in British Columbia and the shootings at Taber, Alberta, and Littleton, Colorado, are just a few high-profile cases.

Yet despite the best efforts of principals, teachers, support staff, parents and students, bullying is still prevalent in schools. It's hard to change attitudes and behaviour, especially when we are immersed in a society that thrives on criticism and judgment.

Isn't everyone entitled to make mistakes and learn from them? It's what makes us human.

I have seen students (and adults!) profess more sympathy for fictional characters on television than they do for the people they come into contact with every day. I find this disturbing – and sad.

When will we learn to appreciate and accept others *because* of their differences? When will we learn not to take offence over some perceived slight? When will we start living by the old adage, "If you don't have anything nice to say, don't say anything at all"?

A group of Grade Sevens recently told one of their teachers that bullying is "a part of life." They also said it "makes you tougher." I strongly disagree. I don't think anyone who has been bullied is grateful for the experience.

Although statistics indicate that most bullies are boys, girl bullying is widespread. Girl bullies generally use exclusion, name-calling and gossip to victimize others, but there are also numerous instances of physical violence.

Thanks to the Internet revolution, bullying is easier, faster and more anonymous than ever. It seems that every techno-logical innovation comes with a perversion of its original purpose. Cellphones and digital cameras have been used to take pictures or video of children in locker rooms and wash-rooms. These images are then uploaded onto websites aimed at targeting the victim. Blogs are used to disparage children and adults. Recently I saw a Grade Twelve student justifying such actions as "freedom of expression."

I have seen numerous presentations, delivered by sincere and eloquent guest speakers of all ages, about the effects of harassment. Reaction to these presentations is generally along these lines: "I really felt sorry for the girl/guy they were talking about. People are so cruel. Somebody should have done something." The bullies promptly resume tormenting their victims because they "deserve it."

I suspect that many teen suicides are connected to homosexuality and bullying. No matter what side of the fence you sit on the issue of gay rights, I think we can all agree that no teenager wrestling with his or her sexual identity deserves to be victimized because of it.

The *good* news – in this increasingly complex world – is that most people – young and old – are horrified by bullying. They are eager to help if given the opportunity.

Here are some simple ways to reduce bullying in your school:

1. Ask yourself, does my behaviour each day make my school better – or worse? How do I want people to remember me when they look back years from now?

2. Say "hello" to every person you meet. Don't make a distinction between who is worthy of your notice and who isn't. Everyone deserves this simple courtesy. Make "small talk" each day with someone to whom you don't normally speak.

3. No matter how tempting, don't spread – or worse, fabricate – gossip. Gossip is a powerful and destructive

addiction, and many people view it as a means to increase their own popularity. Yes, information is power – power that can kill.

4. If you come across someone being bullied, try to distract the bully. Ask a question unrelated to the situation. Change the subject. You don't have to be confrontational to stop the abuse from taking place. Later, urge the victim to report the incident.

If you are being bullied, here are some things you can do:

1. Look the bully straight in the eye and tell him or her firmly and politely to leave you alone.

2. Try not to cry or show you are upset. Bullying is about power. Don't make the bully feel powerful.

3. Talk to an adult you trust.

4. Never give out your password for email. If someone is abusive on MSN, don't respond to the abuse. Block the person and stop accepting their emails. The same applies to text messages.

Here are some resources that might be helpful:

1. Saskatchewan Learning – *Caring and Respectful Schools* (Bullying Prevention Handout)

2. www.cyber-safety.com

3. *Staying Safe in a Wired World* – Rob Nickel

4. *Peacekeepers* – Diane Linden (Coteau Books)

5. www.bullying.org

Remember, any effort to eradicate bullying is worthwhile.

Maureen Ulrich

about the author

Maureen Ulrich was born in Saskatoon, but grew up in Edmonton and Calgary. She has arts and education degrees from the University of Saskatchewan, and has taught middle-years students for twenty-three years, as well as working in the oil field industry. She has lived in Milestone and Lampman, in southeastern Saskatchewan, for the last twenty-seven years.

Although *Power Plays* is her first book publication, she is an avid playwright, having written twenty-six plays for young people, and ten for adults.

MEMBER OF SCABRINI GROUP

Québec, Canada
2007